Praise for Snapshots USA

"Snapshots USA (An American Family Album) is
a heartfelt meditation on the loss of the American
Dream, a dream that died with the murder and
maiming of protesting students at Kent State,
May 4, 1970. Norman Weissman's novel records
every point of view in a country torn apart by fear,
prejudice and hatred in the 1960s and 70s, and
bears witness to the loss of belief in government as
the protector of freedoms and rights under law. A
tale told through the eyes of the student-narrator,
this is a novel that achieves greater truth and moral
clarity than the mere recitation of facts, upon which
the novel is based, could ever hope to achieve. Yet
the facts cannot be concealed forever and in our
collective memory, Weissman believes, lies the path
to understanding, a kind of truth, and the possibility
for national redemption."

Larry Dowler
Archivist, Yale University (1970-1982)
Librarian, Widener Library
Harvard University (1982-1998)

"Snapshots USA (An American Family Album) has a powerful impact as it recalls the Kent State Tragedy isolating and exposing their separate strands into what they really are: Premeditated murder. As Allison Krause's dream burned in a volley of Guardsmen's bullets, the American Dream also went up in flames, in all the media, for all the world to see. Norman Weissman stirs the ashes of that incinerated dream in the pages of his disturbing novel which pricks the American psyche. Forty years have plowed the ashes and rubble under, covering it with new edifices. But as long as artists like Norman Weissman continue writing, the seared spirit of the American conscience will continue to trouble out hearts like the unclean hands of Lady Macbeth."

Paul D. Keane
Co-Founder – The Kent State Collection
Yale University's Sterling Memorial Library
Manuscripts and Archives.

"Snapshots USA is a powerful and disturbing work. A work by the living for the living dramatizing our failure to do justice to the dead Kent State students... The author and his readers are in the company of unquiet ghosts, remembered but neither grieved nor avenged properly."

Paul Shiman, Chairman
Boston Commission on Student Unrest

Snapshots USA
(An American Family Album)

Norman Weissman

Published in the United States by
Hammonasset House Books LLC
64 Edgecomb Street
Mystic, CT. 06255

Cataloging-in-Publication Data is available from
Library of Congress Control Number: 2007943112

History/Fiction

ISBN-13: 978-0-9801894-1-4

FICO: 14000

www.hammonassethouse.com

Printed in the United States of America

In Loving Memory Of:

Allison, Sandy, Will and Jeff.

May 4th, 1970

Prologue

This book is fiction based on fact, fulfilling my obligation to all who told me their stories. Their voices and faces are the pages of our American family album, a record of their humanity.

ONE

The Governor loved press conferences. Enjoyed their intensity heated by blinding lights in overcrowded rooms. Pounding the table, waving his arms, his high-pitched voice welcomed the blinking red eye of the TV camera and shouted questions by reporters shoving microphones in his face. With next week's primary election hotly contested, today's statement could determine his political future.

Today's message was leadership. Showing voters he knew how to take command in a crisis. Master a problem in need of a Final Solution.

"Students are out to destroy higher education," he shouted, when asked why they were demonstrating. "They go from campus to campus terrorizing communities. Sniping at police. They're worse than the Brownshirts or the communist element or the KKK Night Riders or Vigilantes. They're the worst type of people we harbor in America. We're up against the strongest, well-trained, militant revolutionary group ever assembled in America... and we are going to eradicate this problem... not just treat the symptoms."

"And how will you do that?" a reporter asked.

Nodding to the officer at his side the Governor passed the question to the National Guard's adjutant general.

"Ohio law allows us to do anything that is necessary," the adjutant general replied. "Use any force necessary, even to the point of shooting. That's what the law says. Shoot if necessary."

TWO

Our Victory Bell tolled assembly. The bullhorn of a National Guard officer roared the Riot Act as a company of gas-masked guardsmen marched up and over Blanket Hill descending to the athletic field below. Then the guardsmen turned, kneeled, and aimed M1's at us.

"One Two Three Four - we don't want your fucking war!" we chanted.

The sound of exploding gas grenades echoed overhead. Metal canisters trailed dazzling white plumes against a cloudless Ohio sky. A sergeant raised a pistol and fired a shot into the air. The tolling bell hesitated. In the silence a meadowlark could be heard. On the fourth day of May, 1970, we were young, confident, alive chanting: "One Two Three Four - we don't want your fucking war!"

Applause and jeers mocked the guardsmen. The guns, but not the bell remained silent. The soldiers huddled around the sergeant awaiting orders.

We cheered as the formation turned from the parking lot and retreated up Blanket Hill taunted by our derisive laughter. Waving a black flag one student

11

danced a comic jig. Others, fingers upraised, saluted obscenely, chanting:

"One Two Three Four - we don't want your fucking war!"

Other disinterested students strolled to their next class untroubled by bayonet jabbings, clouds of tear gas or shouted obscenities. They saw nothing more threatening than guardsmen shoving demonstrators into their dormitories. As the gas dissipated fear subsided. Flag-waving students shouted: "Pigs off campus! Pigs off campus!" Marching past the pagoda on the crest of Blanket Hill the guardsmen moved beyond range of our rock-throwing arms. As they departed we turned away and glanced at our watches.

12:23 P.M. Time to wash tear gas from our eyes and return to class. Our business here is learning. Not war. Arriving at the pagoda on the crest of Blanket Hill the last rank of guardsmen halted, turned, and with one step back towards the students fired steel-jacketed bullets at the crowded parking lot three hundred yards away. Kent State's "Free Fire Zone." In thirteen seconds four lives were wasted, one student crippled and eight wounded. All shot in the back or side.

A cloud covered the sun as the guardsmen retreated beyond sound of our cries abandoning on the blood-stained ground one dead, three dying, and nine wounded. Ignoring our casualties, the soldiers marched off over the crest of Blanket Hill once known only as a trysting place for young lovers.

THREE

And what is the other side of my story? What did the National Guardsmen see and think and feel when mocking laughter and mindless fear catalyzed confrontation into tragedy? Can anyone understand May 4th 1970 without viewing that incident through a clouded eye shield, cheeks rubbed raw by skin tight gas masks? Without choking, gasping for breath, who can pass judgment? Deliver a fair verdict to a jury of twelve good citizens? And the accused? Weekend warriors. Factory workers. Truck drivers. Blue collar tradesmen struggling to keep in formation, hearts pounding in response to the incessant tolling of an inciting bell. The guardsmen kneel and aim at the parking lot as human targets three hundred yards away appear in their gunsights.

What are our citizen soldiers waiting for? What is happening? Tension builds. Orders are given. Rifles lowered to port-arms, the guardsmen turn and march up Blanket Hill. "Jack and Jill climbed up the hill" a trooper recites to muffled laughter. "Jill fell down and broke her crown" another replies, his voice distorted by a mask filtering out fumes but not the sour, acrid taste of tear gas.

Enraged. Insulted. Humiliated. The guardsmen maintain discipline. Silence. What they really want is to go home.

Perspiring, frightened, they perhaps recall: "Thou Shall Not Kill!" as blurred distant images scream obscenities at them. On the crest of Blanket Hill, at the pagoda, the guardsmen turn and take one step back towards the students and open fire. Without a word of command the platoon turn, aim, and shoot live ammunition at human targets hundreds of yards away. From that day forward images of the dead are embedded in memories. Dark red blood staining the parking lot. A young girl collapsing like a deflated bag of flesh. A student pleading "No! No!" his face shielded behind upraised hands. A supplicant at prayer. Only on this day no prayers are answered. Not for a fatal thirteen seconds. Not ever.

FOUR

Kent State's red brick campus lacked the "Ivy League" look of prestige academia. When our senator remarked Ohio's religions are patriotism and football, we applauded his candor. And when bumper stickers proclaimed "Keep America beautiful, cut a hippie's hair" this imperative was soon replaced by "Kill a Commie For Christ!" inscribing 58,268 names on a remarkable memorial on the shores of the Potomac.

Forensic archives also reveal facts. At the Portage county morgue the taped voice of a coroner recorded undeniable truth.

"Allison B. Krause. Female. Age 19. Penetration of the left lower lobe of lung, spleen, stomach, duodenum, liver and inferior vena cava caused by a 30-caliber military type bullet fired from a distance of 343 feet fragmenting after penetrating the left upper arm and entering the left lateral chest. Massive hemorrhage the cause of death."

"Sandra L. Scheuer. Female. Age 20. Bled to death from a military type bullet fired at a range of 390 feet. Projectile entered the left front side of neck exiting on the right front side severing the jugular vein."

"Jeffrey G. Miller. Male. Age 20. Instantly killed at a distance of 265 feet. A military type bullet entered his mouth and exited at the base of the posterior skull."

"William K. Schroeder. Male. Age 19. On the ground, dead, at a distance of 382 feet. Facing away from the gunfire, fatally wounded by a military type bullet entering his back at the seventh rib with fragments exiting above his left shoulder."

The coroner also noted an M1 bullet fracturing three vertebrae paralyzing Dean R. Kahler from the waist down.

Eighty rounds of steel-jacketed bullets in thirteen seconds. A military response to a peaceful student demonstration.

Nine survived wounds to again watch the black squirrels frolic on Blanket Hill. They heard again the tolling of our Victory Bell wondering why it did not toll for me and thee. And grateful for a future that included wives children and careers, these nine remembered the four who never lived to be twenty-one.

FIVE

On the Oval Office wall a polished brass clock chimed time's relentless syllable. Unredeemable loss. Tonight, seated in a reclining chair at the fireplace, note pad on his lap, pen poised, Our President hoped to write an explanation for tragedy.

Tomorrow's statement required eloquence. Compassion.

He knew about death. Staring into the fireplace he recalled his brother's funeral, the family at the grave, his arm around his father's waist to support an old man's unbearable pain. In a baring of love and grief, father and son swayed back and forth over the pine casket, a sharing of sorrow forever recalled as his rite of passage into manhood.

But yesterday's events were no ritual, no transition to adulthood. Perhaps yesterday's tragedy was inexplicable? Four dead. Nine wounded. One crippled. Throw one stone. Then another. And another. Violence grows. Anger explodes. Death becomes inevitable.

Moving pen across paper he began writing. Dissatisfied, he tore the page from the pad crumpling it into a ball. Again he wrote. Dissatisfied, he crossed out his words with a pen slash. Then an appropriate thought. He printed in large, block letters:

"WHEN DISSENT TURNS TO VIOLENCE IT INVITES TRAGEDY"

Overheard on Main Street:

"The score is four... next time more."
"The Kent State four should have studied more."
"The guards should have shot 'em all."
"Anybody who defied the guard ought to be shot."
"They got what was coming to them."
"Students get away with too much."
"The lazy, the dirty, the one you see out on the street doing nothing... ought to be shot."
"Their bodies were covered with lice."
"The girls didn't wear underwear."
"She was on drugs."
"She was pregnant.
"She was so ridden with syphilis she would have been dead in two weeks."
"She was tattooed from head to toe."
"She was the campus whore."
"They were all dope heads."
"Any damn kid we see with long hair we're going to gun him down."
"They were a bunch of communists."

SIX

"Turn on, tune in, and drop out," a Professor at Harvard University said. And a bearded beatnik poet preached: "Incoherence is superior to precision; ignorance is superior to knowledge; the exercise of the mind and the imagination is a form of death and sordid acts of violence are justifiable a long as they are committed in the name of instinct."

And addressing parents of the despised middle class the popular poet threatened: "We will get you through your children."

SEVEN

Addressing a wildly cheering audience, the assassinated president's brother said: "What we need in the United States is not division; what we need in the United States is not hatred; what we need in the United States is not violence or lawlessness, but love and wisdom, and compassion toward one another, and a feeling of justice toward those who still suffer within our country be they white or black."

The presidential candidate continued, warning about "The mindless menace of violence which again stains our land and every one of our lives. No wrongs have ever been righted by riots and civil disorders. A sniper is only a coward, not a hero, and an uncontrolled, uncontrollable mob is only the voice of madness, not the voice of the people."

And finally the candidate pleaded: "Let us dedicate ourselves to tame the savageness of man and to make gentle the life of this world. Let us dedicate ourselves to that, and say a prayer for our country and our people. Surely we can learn, at least, to look at those around us as fellow men, surely we can begin to work a little harder to bind up the wounds among us and to become in our own hearts brothers and countrymen again.

Some men see things as they are and say, 'Why?' I dream things that never were and say Why not?"

EIGHT

David Constant, attorney, here. Alive and well. A survivor who can not forget. Call me - "A Rememberer." After all, memories are what we are. So we must take good care of them.

Listening to my windows rattling in the wind, the nights are long, the pillows hard. Blankets slide to the floor. Expanding steam hammers radiators. To float free of early morning despair I imagine myself weightless, hovering above my bed. I fly to the far corners of the room searching for intruders. Voices that are no dream.

"I wanted to live," Sandy whispered as her luminous body floated by, auburn hair framing a pale oval face. Lustrous eyes glowed in the shadows. "I wanted to live," she said, "A life worth living."

My heart stuttered a wordless reply.

Outside the window a leafless oak tree creaked. Upstairs a radio blared the Grateful Dead's latest hit. In the street a car back-fired. I heard the strident tolling of a bell; the agony of shrieking voices. With the bilious taste of dread in my mouth I shuddered at my vision of Blanket Hill populated by ghosts.

"How could they forget?" she said. "How could they forget how we died?"

Phantoms danced across my walls. My mind climbed topless mountains, filed briefs with high courts, argued, deposed and pleaded, my heart freighted with remorse. I reached out to touch haunting faces, apparitions, never silent shades. Heard voices I could not deny.

"It was a lovely day," she said, long tapered fingers brushing hair off her face. "A lovely day. Spring. Before the summer's heat. Mud hardened on the walkways. The foliage green. What joy to be alive breathing the goodness of the earth."

She held my hand. I felt a happy regret. Our love. "I'm sorry," she said, "sorry we waited. Now we will never know what our lives would have been."

My heart stopped. She leaned over and kissed me. Gentle as a memory. "We would have had a good life. I know that. That day. Thinking about our future."

I opened my arms. Embraced air.

"Where are the men who killed me?" she asked. "Why was it allowed? I wanted to be a teacher. My parents were proud. A daughter at university. Who would have guessed they'd fire guns we put flowers into? Who would have thought something bad could happen?"

I pressed RECORD, heard the whirr of audio tape unreeling a cassette, watched blinking red lights fail to capture her words. Fated to do battle with time I determined to resurrect the past.

I recall high ceilings, wall-to-wall carpets and oak study tables in the library. Sanctuary from boisterous dormitories. I remember portraits of university presidents on the walls. Weary students pillowed on their arms, napping. Lights dimmed at closing as we crowded the doorway, opening book bags to a cursory glance or an indifferent wave of the monitor's hand.

That was when first we met. She, at the check-out desk, hair pinned back, teasing wide-set eyes. A Mona Lisa smile in washed jeans and baggy wool sweater. Her eyes avoided mine when she turned and stared at my bookbag. She startled me with a laugh.

"This belongs to you," she said, holding my bookbag by frayed shoulder straps. "I found it under the table, next to my chair." Zippers closed, L.L.Bean logos discolored, our bookbags were identical. I opened the zipper and reached into the one she claimed.

"Please!" she said, "that's mine."

I pretended not to hear. Removed a hairbrush.

Sparked by delight her full-throated laugh startled the Monitor. He looked up. "Please!" he whispered pointing to the "Quiet" sign on the wall. "This is a study hall."

We exchanged bookbags. Suppressed laughter.

Outside the library she smiled and said. "I know what was is in your bag."

My mind did inventory. Sweatsuit. Socks. Jockstrap. "I work-out every evening."

"I know. That's how I knew it was yours."

Her look taunted me. I declined embarrassment. "One size fits all, you know."

"Really?"

"Take my word for it."

What begins in delight can end in wisdom. If you have luck. And we had the good fortune of attending classes each day and in the evening, study halls, movies, or romancing on Blanket Hill. Tomorrow seemed a good idea. Careers. Marriage. Family. Yes. The future promised opportunities denied our parents. We had luck. And I have a story to tell. A story worth writing. worth the agony and the sweat. The human heart in conflict with itself.

My imaginings built dreams. Evoked apparitions. Welcomed by my lonely heart, ghosts reopened ancient wounds. Sorrows festered and spread gangrene-like through my soul. I walked the knife-edge of madness. Raised my arms in prayer unable to grasp the image of God. I asked for strength and found weakness, infirmity, poverty of spirit receiving nothing I asked for - but everything I had hoped for. Despite all obstacles, my unspoken prayers were answered.

How? Why? I do not know. Perhaps I should remain mute before the wonder of my story. After all, there is no limit to the stars. And so I tell of memories I am possessed by.

Our together time began in expectation and traversed high promise with no happy ending except she revealed to me the mind behind teasing eyes. She followed the injunction to go forth and bring light to the world; to be "A Servant Candle" assuring the beauty of her better self lived on in minds she touched with fire.

The incendiary flame of language. The fire in words.

Enthralled, she reached into memory. Her voice plaintive. "I loved teaching deaf kids," she said. "How eagerly they learn to speak. Each word a miracle. They're not dumb. Deaf, yes. But not dumb. Never dumb. Smartest kids I ever met. Don't know why they are called dumb when they learn so fast. All it takes is patience and six lollipops. Just six. Ah ay ee ii oo uu. A different color for each sound. Like red is always

Ah. Green is Ay. And so on. Touch a different lollipop to their tongue to teach each sound and it's a miracle how they put sounds together to make words. And the first word they speak is like Christmas morning. Pure joy."

A crimson dawn tinted the sky. Her eyes teared.

"There are some words I would never teach. Never. Words like kill."

NINE

I prayed for a FADE OUT but only a blurred DISSOLVE filled my TV screen. Gunshots. Screams. Sirens. Out of the monitor's clutter emerged an image. A voice. Not what I expected. Not ghostly.

"Where have all the flowers gone?" Allison asked as I pressed the MUTE button. Her image persisted wearing a black dress with a high white collar and long sleeves. She seemed so alive. Same eyes, mouth, lips. She even smiled a little. "Now I know what that song says," she said, her eyes points of light in the shadows. Her face glowing. "I know why we sang that song. Why I remembered the words as my heart slowed until I had no pulse with a fist pounding my chest and someone I didn't know pressing his lips to mine with that final kiss that gives no pleasure. The Kiss of Life they call it but that's not what kisses are for. I want someone I love to kiss me goodbye. Not a stranger."

My finger pressed the OFF button. Allison would not disappear.

"Felt like a truck hit me when that bullet ripped through my arm and lung. Shattered my spleen.

31

Massive hemorrhage the coroner said. Dead on arrival." Her lips moved silently. D.O.A. "My God we screamed. My God!" she said, touching my cheek. "You learn to love life when you're dead. Trees budding in spring. The summer's heat. Fall colors. Faces. My parents. Friends." Her eyes darkened. "There's no love here, you know."

The screen blurred. I wanted no more. I turned and walked to the kitchen. Bright shiny control knobs on the white enamel stove caught my eye.

"Please," I whispered. "You're history." I grasped a knob. Hesitated. Leaning against the stove. A statue carved in ice.

"You look awful," she said.

"Go away," I shouted, thinking: One turn of the knob and she's gone.

"You've lost weight."

"Yes," I said, my fingers touching the promise of that black knob. "There's nothing more to talk about."

She watched me turn the knob. What is death like? I wondered.

"After thirty years?"

Turning the knob to OFF, I said: "I've questioned everyone."

"Not everyone."

"Everyone who would talk," I said, recalling those who maintained a silence more incriminating than words. The silence of consent.

She began to sob.

I fled from the kitchen. Her voice pleading: "Don't look at my autopsy pictures and what the coroner did to determine how I died. Stupid. Worse than when I was shot. Treated me like I was nothing but a piece of meat."

TEN

Jeff's photograph in a cap and gown never worn at graduation was a heart-stopper. Dancing a soft-shoe shuffle, a food tray balanced on fingertips, he made us laugh with a sly wink and happy grin as he tipped his hat to a delighted audience.

A born entertainer.

We loved his songs. Our troubadour in a faded sweatshirt and tattered jeans. Sun-bleached hair tied-back. Pony-tail down to his shoulders. His music made you dance. Some nights, however, his songs drove neighbors to despair. But after that day his room became a shrine. His voice reverberating in the shower a memory some students claimed they could still hear and a few reported seeing him at midnight striding across campus, arms swinging, head down as if butting against a wall.

Could be. If you believe in ghosts.

He was never an apparition until the night his yearbook photograph spoke. I read his lips. "What songs I'd have sung, had I lived," he seemed to say.

"I know," I answered, when I found my voice.

The photograph slowly came into focus. "Is that

33

what they feared?" He asked.

"Yes."

"Is that why they sent in the National Guard?"

"Yes."

His lips formed words I strained to read.

"My songs were such a threat?"

"Yes."

"Songs?"

"They can't win a fight with a song."

Head back. He breathed deep, eyes fixed on mine. Singing: "On Blanket Hill, no flowers grow, among the crosses, row on row."

"There are no crosses on Blanket Hill," I replied.

He nodded. Eyes closed. As if praying:

"If you break faith with we who die, we will not rest, though no flowers grow, on Blanket Hill."

His photograph blurred. And he was gone.

"Now, there are only weeds," I shouted, closing the yearbook.

"Bitter weeds."

ELEVEN

Every evening, after class, Will retreated to a library alcove to fill large notebooks with unreadable script. When not wearing his ROTC uniform he looked like a Ph.D. candidate examining the world through horn-rimmed glasses. And that's what he would have become had he lived. Our political speeches failed to stir him. Friendly, amused, he derided our demonstrations. We were foolish creatures he would write about someday. On a campus roiled by perpetrators and accomplices he was a spectator.

His voice fading, I heard him say: "I wanted to write. I had so many stories to tell. Stories about where my family came from crossing the ocean to settle land my grandparents dreamed of owning. Raising children in sod huts where roofs dripped mud into the soup every time it rained. Stories about kids freezing to death in blizzards. Cows starving in snowdrifts. Babies born on our kitchen table. My grandfather crawling ten miles with a broken leg to find a doctor. Grandmother getting an Indian drunk so he wouldn't burn our barn. Stories I wanted to write had I lived.

I wanted to write about grandfather's Christmas

35

eve in France when the fighting stopped and the soldiers climbed out of the trenches to sing carols to the enemy meeting in 'No Man's Land' to eat and drink and play soccer amidst the barbed wire and shell holes until the generals ordered the guns to open fire so the soldiers would resume killing each other again.

And the next war with stars in our window and how one blue star became gold after a messenger arrived and waited trembling in the doorway before handing my mother a telegram. She put her arms around the sobbing boy sharing a grief great as her own, whispering words I could not hear.

Education was my future, my mother said. And ROTC made college possible. Military studies like Principles of War, Tactics, and Law were fascinating. Knowing the rules of engagement I did not worry when the guardsmen arrived. Orders about lock and load and firing weapons were inviolable. Then, when I heard the first shots I believed they were blanks until a steel-jacketed bullet ripped through my back breaking a rib before exiting my shoulder. Maybe if I wore my ROTC uniform that day I might have lived."

TWELVE

The scattered debris of experience washing on the shores of recognition appear as a series of images like the size and shape of the man seated beside me at the counter of the Water Street diner. He turned to greet me. Extended an enormous hand. A booming voice. A friend to all. Called "Tiny" in jocular tribute to his bulk his smile faded when I showed him the recorder. He hesitated. Thought for a moment about my request. "Press to talk," was all I said.

He grinned. Suppressed a laugh, jowls and chins trembling as he nodded. "I've got nothing to hide," he said, pressing the RECORD button. The red light blinked in response to each word.

"I was on my break in the rear of the garage checking my box to see what I had for lunch. Bologna and cheese. Peanut butter and jelly or some days ham and swiss on rye or whole wheat. I work all night sometimes so I eat good when I can. That day I drove the sweeper all morning. A dirty job. Breathing dust. 'Round one o'clock my boss tells me go to Prentice Hall. Flush the parking lot real good. Turn on the sprinklers and make two or three runs and not just to

37

keep the dust down.

Fifteen or twenty minutes to fill the water tanks. A ten minute drive to the parking lot. Guardsmen blocked the streets but they let me through when they saw it was the water truck. The students were quiet now. Back in the dorms. There were soldiers guarding the burned-out ROTC building when I drove by. I knew something real bad happened before I saw all the blood at the parking lot. Never knew we had that much blood in us. Thirteen bodies bleeding half an hour is a hell of a lot of blood. Come to think about it they held back the ambulances at the barricades 'bout twenty minutes so I guess that accounts for all the blood on the ground."

THIRTEEN

Climbing a flight of granite steps I entered our National Archives. An acolyte admitted to a shrine. Here one finds a record of who we are and what we have achieved. 5 million photographs, 81 million miles of motion pictures, tapes, microfilms, maps, drawing, sketches, paintings, diaries, journals, letters, and newspapers record our history.

In the rotunda, the Declaration of Independence, the Constitution and the Bill of Rights proclaim "What is past is prologue," a promise no truth will be concealed from historians. Obsessed by my quest each discovery yielded new insights. I experienced the passion of a hunter stalking paper jungles on unmarked trails. Each surprise evoked my hunger to know more. I became kin to people I never met. Brother to the dead.

Here are answers to questions I did not know enough to ask.

The man I sought was banished to the basement of a former department store, now a warehouse for documents not enshrined in the main archive.

Here papers of historic interest are evaluated by

an archivist directing them to the furnace or microfilm camera, millions of words selected for immortality or oblivion. To shred or preserve is his choice. "I am a document unfolder," he said. His fingers flattening bundles of paper with a sweep of his hand. "Creases do more damage than damp or heat or the acid in the paper," he explained, his face blue-gray in the florescent light.

He worked quickly flattening each document with a deft sweep of his hand.

Then he looked up from his task and examined the papers I handed him.

He read my request. A 9000 page FBI report. Grand Jury testimonies. Findings of a Presidential Commission. Affidavits. Logbooks.

Interrogations of guardsmen. Freedom of information, our government's pledge of allegiance to democracy was all I asked for.

He shrugged. His eyes turned from the papers to fix on mine. He smiled sympathetically.

"This will take time."

I nodded. "I know."

"You must fill-out a draw-down request for each part of each document describing everything contained in that document."

"A completed form for each part?"

Again he smiled. Impatient. "Yes. All parts included in each document must be itemized. Accurately.

"How is that possible before seeing the document?"

He ignored my question. "Group number, part number, date of request, your I.D. number, signature. Every line on each form must be filled out."

"Then what?"

He paused. Shook his head. Smiling. "Why then you wait."

"How long?"

He returned to the work table. In a measured voice he said: "Sometimes years."

GRAND JURY REPORT
Portage County, Ohio

"Those who acted as participants and agitators are guilty of deliberate criminal conduct. Those who were present as cheerleaders and onlookers, while not liable for criminal acts, must morally assume a part of the responsibility for what occurred.

It should be made clear that we do not condone all of the activities of the National Guard on the Kent State University campus on May 4th. We find, however, that those members of the National Guard who were present on Blanket Hill on May 4th fired their weapons in the honest and sincere belief and under circumstances which would have logically caused them to believe that they would suffer bodily injury had they not done so. They are not, therefore, subject to criminal prosecution under the laws of this state for any death or injury resulting there from.

Although we fully understand and agree with the principle of law that words alone are never sufficient to justify the use of lethal force, the verbal abuse directed at the guardsmen by the students represented a level of obscenity and vulgarity which we have never before witnessed.

Although we fully recognize that the right of dissent is a basic freedom to be cherished and protected, we cannot agree that the role of the vniversity should be to continually foster a climate in which dissent becomes the order of the day to the exclusion of all normal behavior and expression.

What disturbs us is that any such group of intellectual and social misfits should be afforded the opportunity to disrupt the affairs of a major university to the detriment of the vast majority of the students enrolled there. The time has come to detach from university society those who persist in violent behavior. Expel the trouble makers without fear or favor. Evict from the campus those persons bent on disorder."

Respectfully submitted,
    Robert Hastings, Foreman
    October 16, 1970

FEDERAL BUREAU OF INVESTIGATION
REPORT ON KENT STATE
July, 1970

"The campus shooting by the Ohio National Guard which led to the deaths of four Kent State University students was not necessary and not in order. We have some reason to believe that the claim by the National Guard that their lives were endangered by the students was fabricated subsequent to the event."

"The use of gunfire was unnecessary, unwarranted and inexcusable."

John Mitchell
US Attorney General
August 13th, 1971

FOURTEEN

Watching sunset from the crest of Blanket Hill evoked expectations of tomorrow. A promise encouraged by the fragrance of new-plowed farmland. Sitting alone I contemplated a future that promised graduation, a job, and marriage to the girl of my dreams. Looking at the moon I thought about footprints in the dust and our flag planted on a windless crater.

My most vivid memory of May 4th 1970 was a bell tolling. Salvaged from an old steam locomotive, hung in a yoke on a low brick pedestal our Victory Bell assembled students with a strident sound that proclaimed our joy, anger, and a spell of what has been inaccurately described as a riot.

Reverberating across campus that bell charged the air with a current of excitement. Our hearts beat faster as we gathered on the commons to hear impassioned speeches and the angry tolling of that old locomotive bell.

We also heard strident voices broadcasting venomous spite. From the not-so-silent majority we listened to a chorus of vindictive fear evoked by the

Pied-Pipers of our nation's gutter.

Talk radio. Recharging the paranoia of the frustrated. Driven by hatred. Preaching conformity. Striving for omnipotence.

"God Bless America - Love it or Leave it" was their ultimatum to all desecrating the American Dream. A firestorm of hate threatened a "counter-culture" in need of a "Final Solution".

Today my pulse quickens at the sound of a tolling bell. And if you could lick my heart, it would poison you.

Yes, indeed, poisoned by media crap toxic as atomic fall-out. Polluted by lies and half-truths disseminated by TV's ditto heads. And yes, you can rely on stupidity vanquishing truth with life's tragic scenarios recycled as experience. What we never learn from.

Believe me, the lessons I have not learned are legion. Like good will is not always reciprocated. Trying to change people is futile. Playing it safe can be more hazardous than what you fear. And cowardice, petulance, impatience, self-indulgence, self-deceit, living without thought of the future, that's who we are and that's who I am. Or was. Take my word for it.

Did I ever learn? Change? Good question.

Uninvited, the past surfaces like an insurgent army to paralyze days and torment sleep. At fifty-one I'm too old to feel young. Too young to feel old. And too honest to deny responsibility. Thinking. Dammit. Just thinking hurts. After thirty years how does anyone make sense out of senseless deaths?. How do you determine who really pulled that trigger? Identify who created tragedy? Mistrust everyone, widen the generation gap and there's nothing and no one to believe in. Something bad will always happen, says Professor Murphy, and there's not much you can do about it.

I had a lover's quarrel with the good old U.S. of A. Nothing more earth-shaking than that. And yes, I remained silent as too many demonstrating students disparaged, insulted, defamed, and despised Amerika, spelt with a K. Patriotism was politically incorrect. Scorned. But I ask you, is that a crime punishable by death?

I rode no spavined horse on my quest. Only a Subaru of many miles vintage with no Sancho Panza as disciple but only a tape recorder and reels of audio tape as messenger to future arbiters of justice.

Yes, if you could lick my heart it would poison you. Hopefully in the search for truth and justice, an errant knight's impossible dream can be an antidote, transmuting venom into hope.

FIFTEEN

Our President remembered childhood evenings, dishes washed and put way, the family at the kitchen table, his mother reading scripture recalled years later on sleepless nights. "And it came to pass that God tempted Abraham, and said unto him: take now thy son, thine only son Isaac, whom thou lovest, and get thee into the land of Moriah: and offer him there for a burnt offering upon one of the mountains which I shall tell thee of."

Our President turned on the bed light and reached for the family Bible. Opening the worn leather-bound book he read: "One of the mountains I shall tell thee of." He repeated the sentence aloud. Troubled, he wondered: Blanket Hill? A mountain? With trembling hands he read: "And Abraham rose early and took Isaac his son and wood for the burnt offering, and went unto the place of which God had told him. And there on the Third day!" Yes, he said. Yes! May 4th. The Third day. He closed his eyes chilled by the thrall of prophecy. "On the Third day Abraham lifted up his eyes and saw the place afar. And Abraham took the wood of the burnt offering and laid it upon Isaac

his son, and he took the fire in his hand and a knife."
Awed by coincidence he murmured: A fire? A knife?
Bayonets? "And they came to the place which God
had told him of: and Abraham built an altar there, and
bound Isaac his son, and laid him on the altar upon
the wood, and Abraham stretched forth his hand, and
took the knife to slay his son." He closed the Bible.
Thinking. Sacrifice nourishes the tree of liberty. The
time of martyrs may be come again, yet as of old,
no single heart is foul! Who could have anticipated
deadly force would be used? No. Never. Then how
did a show of legal authority result in four fatalities?
How?

"Mr. President," the director replied, his voice
intimate. "My bureau gathers facts." He turned in his
chair, leaned forward, confiding. "Conclusions are the
responsibility of other agencies evaluating evidence
for indictments."

"Cut the crap, Mr. Director," Our President
said. "What do you know that I don't know? What
are you keeping from me when there's no need for
deniability?"

Blood drained from the director's face. His
lips formed a thin line. "I stand by our report Mr.
President," said the director, "Only a Grand Jury can
answer your questions."

Our President pointed at the newspaper on his
desk. "You're wrong, Mr. Director. Wrong. Headlines
decide today's verdicts. Those damn kids are doing to
me what they did to LBJ."

The director glanced at the paper. Eyelids
fluttering. "No way, Mr. President. No way."

"Explain four martyrs. Two of them girls, for
God's sake."

"No one admired those students."

"LBJ couldn't look out the window without hearing Hey! Hey! LBJ! how many kids did you kill today?"

The director shrugged. "Mr. President, we demonstrated what law and order is all about." He removed his glasses. "Everyone applauds your leadership."

"When I want applause, I'll ask for it," Our President said angrily. He rose from the desk. Walked to the window.

"Peace with honor," the director said, turning in his chair. "You have no other choice."

"I'll not be the first president to lose a war."

The director's Buddha-like head nodded. "There is more at stake than your presidency. The Cambodian incursion was just an excuse for students to do their worst."

Our President turned to the director, dark jowls trembling. "What he hell are you saying?"

The Director raised his hand. A manicured finger pointed out the window. "We are confronting outlaws burning libraries and trashing classrooms. Barbarians who want to substitute revolutionary dogma for the rule of law." Our President stared at the clock on the wall. His face saddened, dark thoughts unspoken. He nodded at the director. The director's voice softened. "Our task is to defeat this scourge, and defeat it we will!"

SIXTEEN

To unscramble chattering thoughts a fast drive on a winding road often brought coherence. Not always. Just sometimes. And never on an interstate. Along memory's highway milestones marked my journey to triumph or disaster. Good. Evil. Hope. Despair. Love. Hate. Joy. Sorrow. A slight change of direction made all the difference.

Turning off the interstate onto a county road, inhaling the pungent odor of new-plowed soil I entered a domain free of McDonald's arches. A rural landscape where general stores are post offices and public forums. Here beyond superhighways the song of a meadowlark can still be heard. Here freedom and independence are more than words. And here citizens display a patriotism that often rides the angry steed of paranoia.

My country tis of thee, sweet land of bigotry, of thee I sing. For you made me what I am today. And so you may ask why I wrote so many disturbing letters to a President of the United States.

You've read the headlines. Seen my interviews on TV.

Never abused as a child. Received Dr. Spock's prescribed nurturing. Teachers, ministers, and scout leaders mentored me. Never participated in such juvenile crimes as vandalism, smoking pot, or racing "borrowed" cars after chug-a-lugging a six-pack. Above average in high school. Graduated our State University. Admitted to law school and the bar I determined to make a difference. To be a part of the solution.

My "solution"? Writing to Our President? Yes indeed. I could not stop writing letters to that man. Our leader who showed us the more the soul grows old, the more it fights its fate. The politician who fell from grace is now remembered by his foul mouth, feet of clay and dark unshaven jowls.

Still, I grant you, the man had a point. Amerika with a K was not Nazi Germany. Revolution was not the only possible response to our problems. Not even Dr. Salk could immunize vulnerable disordered and disoriented students from the raging virus of hatred and contempt for everything deemed healthy, decent, or normal. Refusing to take their place in the adult world they despised, too many students were unable to climb out of the hole of failure they dug for themselves. The emotionally bankrupt counter-culture of drugs and sex led nowhere.

Amidst these thoughts I lost my way. Unfolding a roadmap I counted the turns after the interstate. At the next intersection a general store fronted by a hand-cranked fuel pump offered refuge from the high seas of my confusion.

"There's no one with that name roun' here, mister," the storekeeper said, nodding at the rack of mail boxes on the wall. He smiled from beneath the peak of a John Deere baseball cap, cool eyes fixed on mine. "Ain't on my postal route," he said, removing his cap to expose an untanned forehead above a parchment face. He took the map from my hand. "You been wild-goose chasing," he said, showing tobacco-stained teeth. Placing the cap back on his head he pulled the peak down to shield his eyes from a naked light bulb dangling from the ceiling. "Look in the phone book. There ain't nobody by that name 'roun here." He returned the map. "You the police? The FBI? The TV?"

"No."

"Well, our last crime was a stolen pick-up. 'Bout eighteen months ago. Everyone said it was drove into the creek for the insurance." He grinned. "You know, the farmers bank of last resort." He smiled as I showed him the photograph. How he examined the snapshot revealed he was lying. His furtive glance at the familiar.

"Well he ain't got a bad face only he's never been in my store."

He returned the photograph. Innocent eyes. A perjured witness.

"Thank you," I said, and moved towards the door.

"Wish I could help mister. An Army fella, ain't he?"

He knew my man. Name. Rank. And serial number.

"The Guard," I said. "The National Guard."

"Deserter?"

"No."

The storekeeper glanced out the window as a battered pickup parked beside my car. I said nothing. He hesitated. No customer departed his store unsatisfied. He offered me a word of hope.

"It's a big county mister. Keep asking. You'll find

55

someone knows your man."

SEVENTEEN

One fourth of July Our President succumbed to the lure of a carnival's steam calliope parading down Main Street to the county fairgrounds. Watching a barker attract crowds to the "Wheel of Destiny", at the end of the flag-draped midway, he had a startling revelation. Words have incredible power! On this his first job away from home Our President hawked Kewpie Dolls to enthused crowds as a prize for risking half a dollar. His high-pitched drumbeat monologue proved irresistible.

The fair's outstanding attraction was a voluptuous dancer who "walked, talked, wiggled and crawled on her belly like a reptile"; and digging down deep into faded overall pockets for "One thin dime! One tenth part of a dollar!" gaping boys and red-faced men trembled as "Rosita" danced across the stage with a flock of doves, fluttering white wings enveloped in the transparent folds of her flowing dress. In another tent the popular "Coon Ball" game drew a sadistic audience. "Three balls for a quarter!" the barker shouted, his puffed-out cheeks frog-like. "Three balls for twenty-five cents!" he cried as a crowd entered to stare at a large canvas target thirty feet from a countertop covered with baseballs. In the center of the Bulls Eye a young black face grinned, eyes rolling in mock terror. "Hit the Coon! Win an expensive prize!" the barker shrilled, displaying a stuffed Panda bear. "Be a real man!" he cried. "Show your old lady your powerful throwing arm!"

At the target the boy grinned. The crowd hooted and hollered anticipating a bloody outcome. "Three balls for twenty-five cents! Three balls for only a quarter!" the barker shouted as a tall pock-faced youth stepped to the counter, fisted a baseball and carefully aimed at the Bull's-Eye winding up for a powerful pitch.

The boy closed his eyes. The crowd hushed into gleeful silence.

Recalling "Coon Ball" on the midway brought to mind a memory of the naked body of Our President's predecessor emerging from a White House shower dripping wet, cursing, staggering blindly through the bedroom, bent over, one arm reaching out, gnarled fingers groping for a misplaced contact lens. For many months Our President anticipated meeting this president famous for embracing friend or foe. Our President lowered his eyes and turned away. Dismayed.

"Hello there," a familiar voice drawled southern charm. Our President lifted his gaze. His host feigned surprise at encountering a visitor. Huge arms opened in hospitable greeting. Grinning the derisive smile of a "Coon Ball" spectator the tall, unembarrassed president sprawled in an armchair making no effort to conceal over-size genitals displayed as virile tokens of power.

Struck mute, Our President got the message.
"Coon Ball" is the name of the game played in this fucking town.

EIGHTEEN

Denounced for continuing Lincoln's humane treatment of the south, Andrew Johnson confronted a congress that twice introduced articles of impeachment. Seated in an armchair, at two o'clock in the morning, drinking a chilled martini, Our President shared Johnson's dismay that alcohol, sipped slowly, in the final days of a failed presidency can not heal a hurt beyond hurting. He found no comfort in the fact that historians agreed Andrew Johnson's trials were unjust.

Reading Johnson's impeachment transcripts Our President thought about vindication. Perhaps he would go to prison? Great memoirs were written in jail. Nehru. Gandhi. Thoreau in Concord. King in Birmingham. And, the Russians in their gulags. Political martyrs vindicated by writing.

Yes. He paid a price for doing what was right. Couldn't let students screw the country. Always think of the future mother said. Thank God she never saw him resign. And when he's dead and buried - what's to remember? Yes. He'd have one hell of an obituary, no doubt about that.

As he lay dying what would he recall? What would stand out in his fading memory? Would he remember waiting in the rain distributing pink sheets of paper listing his opponents voting record? Shaking hands, asking for votes yet cringing at the touch of a stranger's hand? Would he again see himself interrogating a traitor, bright lights and cameras pounding the drama of his triumph into the consciousness of a nation? Would he remember cartoons showing his dark unshaven jowls emerging from a sewer? Frankenstein rising from the nation's bowels? Yes. The grief and strife of hard-ball politics would never be forgotten. Like his desperate fight against accusations of dishonesty. Or never again trusting that grinning five star general.

He would never forget that night watching strobe light flashes on the overcast studying his plexiglas reflected image. For the first time he saw his face aged. Showing strain. Worried. Yes indeed, a damaging allegation. The media predicting his political demise. Well, it never happened. The intercom sputtered interrupting the thought. A garbled voice announced fifth in the traffic pattern. Thirty minutes to the gate. The stewardess refilled his glass.

Military heroes should stay out of the Oval Office. Disasters. Every one of them. Jackson. Tyler. Harrison. Grant. Failures. He raised his glass. The stewardess set another bottle on the tray. The jet banked and plunged into the clouds. Withdraw, his political advisors insisted. Quit! But hell, one false scandal does not a resignation make. Seems the general never heard of the presumption of innocence. Well one speech on TV hit a home run. Bases loaded. Still that philandering hypocrite refused to endorse his running mate.

He closed his eyes. Answered all charges with that spineless general holding a finger up to the wind. Well, a hurricane of phone calls and telegrams told him which way the winds were blowing. Yes indeed. That's something he'd never forget.

Rain-soaked banners decorated the terminal. The whine of jet engines competed with the band's triumphal "March of the Gladiators." The cheering crowd banished images of depressing hotel rooms. Bad meals. Sleepless nights. Blinded by dazzling lights he waved to the cameras. Exhilarated, he paused in the doorway to savor the delirium of campaigning, arms raised, fingers spread in a "V" for victory salute. He held this pose as the bright lights and TV cameras evoked an exultation, a lifting of his spirit that he held on to for as long as possible. Yes. He was a winner. A winner! A moment to remember, by God.

Waiting on the tarmac, the general lifted his hat, arms open, spectators shouting approval as he stepped forward to embrace the prodigal candidate returned to the Party's ethical fold.

"That's my boy!" the general shouted. "That's my boy!" he repeated as the cameras zoomed in and the band played "The Stars and Stripes Forever." "That's my boy!" the crowd chanted to acknowledge reconciliation.

Trapped in the general's enfolding arms, head resting on his shoulder, Our President's joyous moment of triumph aborted, months of anguished humiliation evoked heart-rending sobs as the television lights darkened and the jubilant spectators fell silent.

Yes, Yes. Yes. Life is nothing but trouble when you fight for what you believe. Hated. Detested. Scorned.

Worth all the shit if at the end you can say - win or lose: I have done my best for my country.

How you play the game and what stakes you play for - that alone reveals who you are.

NINETEEN

Who can deny that guns, traffic accidents and psychotic rage produce an annual death toll as commonplace as a weather report?

With so many killed every day, what's one more?

A tedious statistic?

Can we ever understand the impact of one death?

I turned on my tape recorder. The mother acknowledged the blinking red light. She reached up to smooth strands of gray hair tied back in a silver comb. "Nobody called to explain what happened or say they're sorry," she said. "It was only the TV told me my girl was no more."

Behind the house a children's swing trembled ghost-like in the wind.

"The phone rang," she recalled. "Friends asked could they help? Help? My child's gone. Can you bring her back?" She turned and stared out the window at the gently swaying swing.

"I can still hear her shouting Higher Mommy! Higher! Oh how she loved that swing. Never afraid."

She turned and faced me. I looked away.

Discomfited.

"Why was she killed?" She looked down at the ground. Her head nodding. "Nobody's to blame, they said." A silent pause, hands trembling, she smoothed wrinkles in her thin cotton dress. "Nobody's at fault, they said. No one. Not the general. Not the Governor. Not the President of the United States." She touched her breast. "Who will heal this pain?" she asked. She looked out the window at the swing suspended from a tree. Thinking. Remembering. "Hatred's poison. People laugh and are happy and you hate them because you're so miserable."

She reached out. Touched my hand. "Once I believed we were a great country. Raised my daughter that way. Then we went to court and watched our government bend the truth. Kill four innocent students to teach a lesson. My girl died to teach other students a lesson."

She closed her eyes.

"Strangers phoned calling my baby a Jew communist bitch saying she got what she deserved. Told me she was a whore. Diseased. Threatened to burn down our home if we insisted on suing the government. You know how Jews are, they said, all they're interested in is money. Blood money. Well, what we want is justice. When we visit our daughter's grave what do we say? Do we say there is no justice? Do we say no one cares you are dead? That you were executed? Will we ever be able to tell her justice has been done? That the truth has been told?

Someone wrote saying too bad only four got killed. Should have killed forty. Neighbors who knew our daughter from the day she was born said my husband was a traitor. He who fought Hitler and was decorated for courage. Next morning he went down to the basement and threw all his medals in the furnace. It wasn't enough to kill our child, they tried to destroy our pride."

She hesitated. Remembering. "My daughter's smile brightened every day. No one can forget her smile. And her laugh. And they put out her light. Silenced her laughter and it was only after fighting in court ten years the state of Ohio wrote a letter of regret and awarded the families of the children they killed fifteen thousand dollars. Fifteen thousand dollars for the life of a child."

TWENTY

Lucky Lincoln. He had a good war to fight.

At dusk, staring out his bedroom window at the tents and camp fires on the muddy fields between the White House and the Potomac, Abraham Lincoln heard the singing of the regiments waiting to march on Richmond. Tormented by a war he could not prevent, vexed by burning cities and draft riots, enduring a hostile press, Lincoln refused to accept defeat. With a wool shawl over his shoulders he shivered in the night air as he prayed for a general willing to fight. Climbing into his oversize bed Lincoln prayed for a night's sleep uninterrupted by a dream.

Muffled drums rolling.

Four soldiers. Honor guard at a catafalque bearing a flag-draped coffin.

A line of silent mourners.

A woman sobbing.

Lincoln asked who died. The drums stopped beating. "The President," a sorrowful voice replied. He awakened, night clothes soaked in sweat.

A century later, Our President, chilled by another dream, awakened. Rising from his bed he walked to the window to listen to the singing of demonstrators on the Mall their protest now gentled by fatigue. Besieged in the White House he strained to understand what was happening.

In the humid summer air of that Potomac night he recalled the fragrance of California orange groves, the sharp tang of Eucalyptus wood smoke thickening the morning mists. Our President thought about his sainted mother and a father hardened by financial failure; the cruelty of one night's frost destroying a harvest, the drudgery of storekeeping offering only a future of endless struggle. Life's hard lesson. Staring out the window at the students on the Mall he wondered what they knew about hardship.

As one day in Caracas, trapped in a narrow street under a hailstorm of rocks pounding his limousine he defied other students screaming "Yanqui Go Home!" Staring out shattered windows at faces contorted by hate he wanted to confront their fury and demonstrate that yes, he was also a man of courage.

In that battered limousine he discovered he was not afraid of death.

Cut by glass shards, restrained by bodyguards, he struggled to get out of the car to confront the mob armed only with words. Words were his weapon of choice. Long lines of words, marching and counter-marching before hostile audiences rescued him before.

Tonight, staring out the White House window he recalled that narrow street blocked by a stalled truck, the attacking demonstrators, and his futile effort to explain his visit. He had come to do more than place memorial wreaths on monuments. It was right that he do this and who can doubt that doing right is the right thing to do? As on this night there was no doubt he was right and the protesting students in their brightly colored tents on the mall, wrong. Consummately wrong.

At one-thirty in the morning he summoned his valet and dressed, determined not to miss another opportunity to explain himself.

TWENTY ONE

"As lovely a land as ever lay outdoors" said author Sherwood Anderson describing his beloved Ohio. From the fertile bottom land beyond the Appalachians to the grass-covered western plains homesteaders ploughed the prairie to create a legacy for their children. In a Dayton bicycle shop man's dream of flight became real and on the waters of Ohio's great lake freedom was defended under a flag that proclaimed: "Don't Give Up The Ship!".

Today, Ohio's cities are blighted by burned-out slums and uncollected garbage. Shabby rows of tenements with plywood covered windows display the graffiti of urban despair. Driving down avenues of abandoned stores I thought of the expectations that once energized this squalor now blockbusted to foreclosure and decay. Gone forever are generations of family pride that scrubbed these now crumbling wooden porches; gone and unremembered the joy of washing windows, hanging starched curtains above now unpainted window frames.

I sought my man among the homeless in alleys and culverts; outcasts huddled under bridge abutments or in shacks insulated by flattened tin cans. I roamed an America of cast-offs, dope-heads and crazies who survive without food stamps or welfare checks. Casualties of a war called "urban renewal," the homeless are human litter, an intractable problem in logistics, camouflage and waste disposal.

Driving down Commonwealth Avenue through a neighborhood of once prosperous stores I stopped at a red light as a ragged squad of windshield washers with buckets, polishing cloths and rubber squeegees surrounded my car. Cranking down the window I gave a dollar to a bearded veteran wearing a combat jacket his face obscured behind white soapsuds. With a deft sweep across the glass he wiped my window clear. I recognized he was my man. The one I was searching for.

Chilled by a cold rain blowing in from the lake, sickened by the putrid odor of burning soft coal, I needed a drink. A bar and grill seemed just the place to wash away the sour ghetto taste. I went inside and sat in a booth at the rear and ordered coffee.

The Bartender shouted to the kitchen. A reluctant waitress shuffled towards me, cup, saucer and creamer in hand.

I drank the coffee aware of the Bartender's furtive look into the mirror behind the bar. He had me tagged. Even the TV monitor turned away. Then to my surprise the not welcome sign vanished as my man came in and sat opposite me. Wearing an unkempt beard and an old army jacket this man's name was Outrage. Or maybe Despair. Who knows? There's never been an honest body count for our walking wounded.

"How about a drink?" he asked opening his

jacket, cold fingers fumbling oversize buttons. "How'd the hell did you find me? I'm not exactly 'News of The Day.'"

"Maybe you're news that stays news."

"What's that?" he said turning to greet the waitress as a whiskey and beer arrived. Frostbitten fingers embraced the mug. "Kent State happened a lifetime ago."

" I know."

"Twenty-eight years."

"Thirty."

His head snapped back as he swallowed the whiskey. Then, a sip of beer. "What's in it for me?" he asked. "Why should I talk to you?"

"To tell your story."

Hesitating. Unembarassed he asked: "How about money?"

"There's none."

"Well we joined the guard for the money." Raising the mug he suppressed a tight-lipped laugh.

"What's funny?"

"Money. For vacations or cars."

"How much?"

He shrugged. Then, laughing: "Twelve-eighty a day one weekend a month and two summer weeks on maneuvers."

He waited my response. I refused to smile.

"Draft boards left us alone 'cause we were serving Uncle Sam stateside."

"And not in Vietnam."

He nodded. Remembering. "Back then the unions had big balls, weren't afraid to strike and we got ordered out a lot. Nothing much happened except some guys throwing rocks at us when they had one too many."

The waitress set another round on the table.

Again he raised his glass without wishing anyone long life. "With students it was different." He stared into the mug. "Like when you went to a bar guys slapped you on the back and told you what a great job you did and how students got what they deserved and how come you only killed four of the draft-dodging bastards."

He raised the beer mug. His chalice?

"You got treated like you were a hero only you never felt heroic."

He drained a bitter cup.

"Everybody asked how many did I kill? And when I told them I never fired a shot nobody believed me. Troopers who said they only fired into the air or at the ground weren't believed. I never shot nobody. But that's not what everybody wanted to hear and I couldn't convince them I never shot anyone."

His face hardened.

"Only five troopers admitted they shot students. Only five! And we had to back them up. It was a fucking lie about firing in self-defense. From the Governor on down we've had to back up their bullshit."

He looked around for the waitress. Raised his glass. She stepped out from behind the bar. Another round.

"My wife never asked questions and when I tried to talk about it she didn't want to hear what happened. I could never explain how we couldn't stop some troopers from shooting. We never talked about I never killed nobody. She didn't believe I never fired a shot. So it was never the same between us after that day and if you keep asking around you'll find a lot of divorces in Troop G of the Ohio National Guard."

TWENTY TWO

Driving down Constitution Avenue to the mist shrouded Lincoln Memorial Our President recalled the union regiments bivouacked on the mall. He envisioned Lincoln in a long black coat and tall hat trudging through the mud to speak with soldiers soon to face death at his command. He shared Lincoln's belief that old men sending the young to war should do so reluctantly.

On this night exhausted students bedded down before that brooding statue as if expecting Lincoln to lighten the burden of another terrible war. Our President resolved that if this conflict is called his war then the peace that follows would also bear his name. Peace with honor.

He climbed the memorial steps accompanied by Secret Service agents scanning a crowd that recognized his dark unshaved jowls. He hoped to explain how yesterday's Cambodian incursion would bring peace.

Blankets draped around shoulders, the students shivered in the cold morning mist. Our President explained he came to hear what they had to say. Dissatisfied with his rambling monologue about baseball and California surfers the students returned to their sleeping pads.

Our President was no Abraham Lincoln.

Behind the Capitol dome the morning sky brightened. The Secret Service cleared a path to his car. Bleary-eyed demonstrators stepped back and jeered. Several waved farewell. Our President paused at the limousine door, turned and raised both arms, twin V's of upraised fingers silhouetted against the sky. Prolonging this pose a moment he entered the car and grinned at the students through tinted bullet-proof glass.

A tall demonstrator, a red bandana covering sun-bleached hair emerged from the crowd to suddenly turn with a swivel-hipped feint reversing direction to break through the protective cordon of bodyguards. Flushed with triumphal joy he ran after the departing limousine, one hand thrust forward, a finger upraised in obscene salute.

Our President stared out the window and with a smile raised the middle finger of his right hand to return the insult.

TWENTY THREE

Turn on a tape recorder and what do you get from a witness? Hesitation? Fear? Or merely regret? Unwelcome questions elicit dubious answers. Few admire a "Snitch" and one unanticipated payment for informing is contempt. Thank God we don't live in a country where every third person is a police spy. Husbands and wives, and even your best friend reporting thoughts and behavior stored in unevaluated "Raw Files", retrieved and exploited as weapons of intimidation. Trust and decency are casualties when governments make war on citizens.

At the security desk the guard opened my recorder and examined the mechanism. He looked surprised.

"Sure make them small," he said, inserting my visitor's pass into the time clock. "One hour," he announced, returning my I.D. "You his Lawyer? Family?"

"No."

"Well, one hour, that's all. When I say go, you go."

I nodded.

He admitted me into the visitor's hall. From behind a wired glass window my man waited, his bloated face grayed by the pallor of confinement.

"Thanks for seeing me."

"Why not?"

"Where should we begin?"

"How about with my gun?"

I turned on the recorder. Set the volume. Nodded.

He hesitated. Gates of memory parting. Without a smile he said: "The gun was only for my protection. Everybody said I was an informer, you know. Photographing the crazies parading around campus was all I ever did. "He stared at the blinking red recorder light. Remembering. In a hushed voice he said: "The Feds paid me for my pictures. That's all. Other students informed on the demonstrators."

He stared at the recorder. Palms up. Explaining.

"Couldn't let our school go down the drain. There's more than one way to serve our country. Taking pictures for the Feds was my way."

A suddenly old man. His face saddened.

"After that day I had nothing but trouble." I signaled him to wait. Turned the cassette over. When the blinking light resumed he said: "I told myself what's so bad about working for the Feds? That was before they treated us like we did something wrong. Never knew the guns had live ammo. The previous week in Cleveland strikers threw more rocks at the guard than the students did and the soldiers never fired a shot."

His eyes closed. An image clouded his mind. "They could have arrested the leaders. But it was like they wanted a riot and when it didn't happen they opened fire anyway. Four dead or forty. Who gives a damn."

"Many do."

"Do what?"

"Care about what happened."

After a pause, unfazed, he went on. "The Grand Jury indicted 24 students and a professor. After I testified I got dumped like an old whore they fucked real good. We all got dumped by the Feds like we were an embarrassment.

"You were."

He nodded and said: "I felt like the informer in that movie facing a jury with nobody saying a word and me sitting there sweating blood and seated in the front row of the jury box staring at me were the four students killed that day and coming down the aisle in a wheelchair, the one who was paralyzed. The Prosecutor. And when I'd wake up and stop shaking I'd know for sure I gave something of myself to the Feds and what's more, I knew I'd never get it back again. Ever."

TWENTY FOUR

Our President could not escape the rhythmic pounding of the surf. Battered by the explosive fury of the sea the beach trembled beneath his feet as the haunting cry of seagulls proclaimed mortality. Lonely walks along kelp-strewn sand failed to comfort a mind that lost confidence after resigning office. Fleeing hostility he inhabited an imagined purgatory of unknown hazards silhouetted against threatening skies. Shadows concealed assassins. Stalkers lurked the dunes. Secluded in his oceanside home he sought refuge in a long illness, the days threatened by slanted shadows rising in the dark corners of his room. Time was marked by the sound of rubber-wheeled carts rumbling over hardwood floors, food trays clattering on serving tables, voices awakening him with "How are you today, Mr. President?" Time became abrasive voices and blinding lights and when the lights darkened shadows appeared in a frightening void. Recovering he returned from a domain of blurred voices echoing thru passageways that brightened when he opened his eyes. Awakening he returned from illness to try to understand lost weeks, months, could it be a year?

A face framed in gray appeared. Astonished, he recognized a maternal smile. "How are you this morning, my son?" she asked. "Sleep well?" A serving table slid beside his bed. He lowered his eyes to examine the food tray.

"You must eat," his mother said propping a pillow under his head. "You need your strength," she insisted, her lips compressed in a thin line of worry.

"I am not a crook," he said, restraining tears. "You believe that, don't you mother?"

She stared at him surprised. "Yes, my son," she nodded. "You are not a crook."

He glanced at the tray. Unshaven jowls darkened. Confusion blurred thought. He whispered. "I never was a crook. Never."

She reached out. Caressed the stubble on his cheek. Nodding, she said, "I know. And so do your friends. So eat. Get back your strength."

"Now I am disarmed," he mumbled.

His mother strained to hear. "What? my son" she asked. "What did you say?"

A nurse entered opening the blinds. Shadows dissolved. He wondered, am I dreaming? Dazzled by sunlight he closed his eyes.

"What did you say, my son?"

"Liars, scoundrels, they all betrayed me."

An insistent voice paged a doctor. A crackle of static answered. They looked up at the loudspeaker expecting more.

"Yes," she said, nodding. "I understand."

He suppressed tears. His head throbbed. "I am not a murderer. Never ordered anyone killed. Never. Never did what they accused me of."

"Please, eat."

He pushed the tray aside. "The students attacked Police. Killed judges. Burned buildings. Threatened to assassinate me!"

"A heavy burden my son," she said, her face suddenly old. A lived-in look. Yet how young she seems. How young.

"They tried to destroy universities. Our government. And I stopped them. I stopped them."

"You did what was right."

"I did what a president must do."

"Man born of woman is of few days, and full of trouble."

He fell silent. "I am not a crook," he murmured.

"The righteous are in the hands of God and no torment shall touch them."

"I am not a crook" he insisted, his eyes tearing.

"In the sight of the unwise their departure is misery, and their going destruction; but they will find peace."

"I hope that is true."

"Believe and it will be. Now my son, eat. You need your strength!"

TWENTY FIVE

Removing scabs of denial from unhealed wounds proved unsatisfying. Obsessed with our dead I inhabited a purgatory of shuffled papers, dictated briefs, transcribed depositions and probated wills missing dates and misspelling names. Stumbling through the pastures of the law I sowed chaos. Fleeing my office, I traveled as often as possible.

On a hill above the Hudson river, overlooking the Palisade's granite bluffs, the red tiled roof and stone walls of Maryknoll seminary blended spiritual power with oriental mystery. The Seminarian greeting me in the doorway wore the prescribed uniform. Black shirt buttoned at the throat. No necktie. Gray sweater worn at the elbows. He watched me enter the visitor's lounge raising a hand in greeting. Though tense and wary, this soft-spoken young man sat down and nodded graciously before answering my questions, his eyes revealing that not all of May 4th's casualties occurred on Blanket Hill. Hesitating, he turned and looked out the window. The "thousand yard stare" of someone who had seen too much of death. I fumbled with the volume control of my tape recorder waiting for words to surface on an upwelling surge of uncontrolled feeling before turning on my red blinking light.

He seemed surprised by what he had to say.

"My father's closet hid the terrible secret that shattered our family. I was looking for a necktie on the rack behind the door when I discovered his guardsman's uniform. He tried to conceal he had been on Blanket Hill that day.

"Not every trooper opened fire."

"I did not know that. Then." He studied his hands. Fingers extended. Fists opening and closing.

"After discovering the truth silence became the language we spoke. Silence his only response to my questions."

The Seminarian turned to look out the window. In the river valley a train, air horn wailing a doppler cry, raced by.

"When he knew I knew, something died between us. Something he needed that I could never give him while he was alive."

"And what was that?"

"Forgiveness."

He held his hands out, palms pressed together, remembering. "I woke that morning and heard my mother calling my name. Which was also my father's name. Her sobbing voice carried up stairs from the kitchen calling our name. I wondered what I had done to hurt someone who never shed tears for wounds inflicted by angry words and the silence of a troubled marriage. She cried no tears for hurts beyond consolation. Never. But this morning, going downstairs to the kitchen, I heard my mother calling my name. Which was also my father's name."

His eyes stared past me. Into horror.

Then, "What a strange dream I said to myself hesitating in the doorway, seeing my mother bent over the stove. Confused, choked by the pungent odor of gas, I could not walk into the kitchen. I could not take a few steps to comfort my mother. So it was I saw, seated in a chair, head resting on the white enamel surface of the open oven door, my father who heard nothing, the man I could not forgive forever silent continuing as his only legacy the pain-filled silence that was the only language we spoke to each other. After that day on Blanket Hill."

TWENTY SIX

Nothing can poison a night's sleep like a bad dream. And indeed, pollute the day that follows.

The Congressional Doorkeeper strutted down the aisle, head back, announcing Our President's entrance. This night, in this vivid dream, the doorkeeper's booming voice could not be heard. No formal greeting resonated the chamber walls. No applause, cheers, or cries of approval greeted Our President walking unescorted to the podium. Blinded by TV lights he looked up into a blur of unfriendly faces.

He recalled other triumphant parades down this aisle, outstretched hands reaching to grasp his as he moved through a jubilant audience impeded by their enthusiastic embraces. His distinguished escorts' smiles radiated political power as they accompanied their guarantor of future victory to the podium. Walking slowly down the aisle they prolonged this tumultuous demonstration of their mandate. Tonight, in this dream, entering a now silent chamber unescorted, Our President stepped up on to the podium where black-robed supreme court justices refused to rise from their seats and shake his hand.

The Prosecutor looked up at the visitors gallery and out at the audience. "My friends," he began, his words building an indictment with each sentence, "Our government is the ultimate teacher of good or evil. Teaching by example. If our government breaks the law it breeds contempt for the law inviting every citizen to become a law unto himself. When our nation is divided, with rising tensions that may explode at the slightest provocation, enforcers of the law respond to attitudes displayed by their political leaders. Enforcers of the law also respond to the violent mood of the citizens they have sworn to protect. Influenced by inflammatory speeches, confronted by lawful demonstrators seen as the 'enemy,' inadequately trained in riot control, insulted and jeered at, confronted by what they believe was a deadly threat to their lives the guardsmen opened fire. Only on this day their actions were not a scene in a stageplay or TV Show. Nor can we call the deaths that occurred a tragedy that had to happen. These deaths were not an inevitable accident pre-determined by destiny. These deaths were an unlawful response to a legal protest with gunfire. The killings were executed by men with responsibility for what they did. If we are truly committed to the rule of law and our concept of justice these events must be called by their right name -- murder."

TWENTY SEVEN

Robbie was Kent's most powerful lineman, one of our "seven blocks of granite". A big guy. An unforgettable laugh. A man to admire. Born in Cleveland. Father unknown. Mother a nurse. Straight-A student. Stoked frat house furnaces to pay tuition. Won a scholarship to Harvard law. Then a New York law firm hired him. Outstanding record as a district attorney. Appointed a federal judge with his opinions printed in law reviews. His oak-paneled office displayed signed photographs of three presidents he served. On a table behind his desk a most valuable player trophy reminded me of screaming crowds rising to their feet as he swivel-hipped down the field to score a winning touchdown. Now behind his desk he seemed larger than I recalled. Still solid muscle under all that black flesh.

"Thirty years too soon," he said, pausing as a random thought defined itself. "Historians never get it right."

I hesitated. Studying his face. Uncertain of my welcome. Then, blunt, I asked: "What do you recall about May fourth?"

Startled, he turned to look out the window. A long silence. Then, turning to me, there was no smile.

"I recall telling our brothers and sisters - get off campus! Get off campus! When the Guardsmen come - Go home! Go home! We'd watched riots on TV. Watts, Chicago, Cleveland, Newark, Detroit, Orangeburg, Jackson State, Southern. It didn't take much to convince blacks to leave campus so that's why not one got hurt. Not a one. You know, when guns come on campus even lily white's not safe."

I waited. He nodded. Remembering.

"Students convinced there was no danger got shot. A hell of a way to learn hatred's color blind."

I remained silent.

"What happened was photographed. Hundreds of pictures. TV Films. Thirty eye-witnesses. Despite all that evidence the Grand Jury saw only what they wanted to believe had happened. Students rioting. A legal response by the National Guard to danger."

He turned to look out the window. Shrugged. "If what you're looking for is a riot and a deadly threat that's all you will see. What's in your bigoted head from the day you were born."

TWENTY EIGHT

Was the exhaustion of a political campaign prelude to a nervous break-down? To sleepless nights? Rootless fatigue? Unrelieved dread and a tantrum impatience with frustration? Despite his disdain for "Shrinks" Our President visited a therapist famed for helping executives who only regret they have but one life to lose for success.

The Psychiatrist nodded, scribbled a few notes and spoke in an accented voice tinged with regret. Looking up from his writing pad he focused on the abstract painting behind Our President's chair.

Visiting his therapist's office, Our President, troubled by disturbing dreams and a hostile press stared out the window at a willow tree in the garden sprouting the first buds of spring. An encouraging sight in a city that never properly welcomed him.

"Well?" said the Psychiatrist, writing on his note pad, "You've had a another difficult week."

"You can say that again Doc."

The therapist turned to glance out the window. "To me you seem as resilient as that tree."

"The original Comeback Kid," Our President

said, pride in his voice. A boastful laugh.

The doctor scribbled on his pad. "Seems a comeback is something you can be proud of."

"It's no fun, Doc. Believe me."

The therapist lowered his eyes. Turned a page. "A second chance is always a welcome event."

"Like in the Book of Job?"

Startled, the doctor raised an eyebrow. "Never thought of Job that way."

"Neither God or the Devil defeated him, you know."

The doctor paused. Searching a response. "Yes, come to think of it, Job was resilient."

"More. Much more. Think about Job, Doc. Think about how God and the Devil conspired to destroy him."

Taken aback, the doctor laid his pen down on the notepad and stared at Our President. A questioning look.

"A conspiracy?"

Silence. Our President hesitated.

"Yes Doc. A conspiracy."

"What makes you say that?"

"Well most stories are make-believe, Doc. Make-believe. Only Bible stories are for real."

The therapist lowered his eyes. Suppressed a thin-lipped smile. Turned the page of his pad. Writing.

"Think about Job's misfortune, Doc. Job had everything until God boasted to Satan there's none like Job, an upright man who fears God and rejects evil."

The doctor turned another page.

"Take away all Job has," Satan told God, "and he will curse you."

"Then you believe in Satan?" the doctor asked,

restraining excitement. Suppressing a smile.

"Satan's everywhere, Doc. In everyone."

Surprised, the doctor closed his eyes troubled by unstated thoughts.

"Tormented by boils Job refused to curse God and cried out let the day perish when I was born. My soul is weary of life. Me, a just and upright man scorned by family and friends. Mocked. They whom I loved turned against me."

Our President rose from his chair and stepped to the therapist's desk. His voice, his face, exultant.

"You see, Doc, Job never did curse God and God regretted all that he done to Job and gave Job twice as much as he had before so Job died old and full of days. Now that's some comeback story, Doc. One hell of a story."

The therapist nodded. Bemused.

"And Doc, if Job can comeback after what he endured - So can I! Don't you agree?"

TWENTY NINE

These words are common property. A community of words that belong to everybody. And I continue writing until there is no more to be said. For writing is a communion and my remembering keeps the future unbroken with the past.

Overwhelmed by audiotaped interviews I ask: what do these words signify? What do they mean? What distortions have I inflicted on truth when I edit, selecting conflicting visions of a tragic event? I have taken a long painful walk around my subject and here poor fool with all my lore I stand no wiser than before.

It is enough to drive a man to drink, so when you need some small talk and a tall beer see your friendly bartender. Troubles are less daunting when you reflect on your past in his company. Many bartenders chatter non-stop. Others dwell on thoughts as painful as your own for they also have failed dreams, thwarted ambitions and unpaid bills. This bartender answered questions as he dried beer mugs with a small towel.

"Closing bars on Saturday night was just plain stupid. Keeping students off the streets would have been real smart. And moving the curfew back an hour made hanging-out downtown illegal. Only most students were never told about the change in time.

Never saw looting. Or a riot. Students were pissed-off when the bars closed. Out in the street they raised a little hell like on a football weekend. Then the guard comes in from Cleveland where they'd been on duty all week. What the troopers needed was to go home and get some sleep. Ten days active duty is too long when you're newly married or have a girl you're not too sure of. They'd been shot at in Cleveland you know. Strikers threw stones at them. All the guard wanted now was a few days R and R.

Monday, May 4th, lunchtime. Waiting tables at the Brown Derby while the troops marched up and down Blanket Hill like they rehearsed the day before only now they're reading the Riot Act to students tossing gas canisters back and forth with that goddamn locomotive bell tolling like the world's coming to an end.

When the shooting began my customer was ordering lunch like he had nothing else on his mind. Kids dying on Blanket Hill while our university's president studied the menu with me wondering how can he have any appetite at a time like this?"

THIRTY

Of all the portraits in the White House Our President most admired Teddy Roosevelt's. A man of discipline, character and will. On sleepless nights, wandering darkened corridors, Our President recalled the asthmatic boy in his father's arms fighting for breath later restored to health as a cowboy in the Dakotas. Author, hero, Nobel prize peacemaker, canal builder, hunter, explorer, devoted husband and father, Roosevelt's portrait often spoke to Our President clearly audible despite the rumble of street traffic and jets passing overhead.

"Six crises are insufficient," the portrait said. "For one daring greatly, abused by critics, six crises are an apprenticeship. You haven't won your spurs, been really tested until you've survived sixty!"

Our President fell silent, his response unstated. He stepped back from the painting evading the "Rough Rider's" famous glaring eyes.

Roosevelt continued: "I could paper the Oval Office with telegrams received every year. Famine in Africa. Revolution in Panama. War in Asia. Not a day of peace."

Our President heard and nodded. Yes. Peace without honor was unacceptable.

"I dreaded telegrams," the portrait said. "Telegrams announced disasters."

Our President lowered his gaze. "I know about disasters," he said. "I've had more than my share."

"Well, have you ever had really bad news?" the portrait asked. "Catastrophes like the day I received a telegram asking me to come home immediately. I rode the train cursing the miles between me and my beloved wife Alice. The worst day of my life."

Our President stepped back from the portrait to end the conversation. He felt awkward conversing with a painting.

"In the doorway of my home," the portrait continued, "my brother Elliot's face foretold disaster. Mother is dying, he said. Alice is dying too he cried, embracing me, sobbing. There is a curse on our house, he mumbled. A terrible curse on our house!"

Our President chilled. Was he with his troubles accursed as well?

"Our family's afflictions. My asthma. Father's cancer. Elliot's drinking. Mother killed by typhoid an hour before my dear wife Alice died from an inflammation of the kidneys no doctor suspected. What could cause this cruel fate?"

Our President remained silent thinking of his own misfortunes. Yes. Destiny is an enigma.

Then in a hushed almost inaudible voice Roosevelt said, "No loss is greater than the death of a loving and devoted wife, beautiful in face and form, and lovelier still in spirit; as a flower she grew, and as a fair young flower she died. And when my heart's dearest died, the light went out my life forever."

THIRTY ONE

At rural country stores few patrons disclose a neighbor's name. Or where they live. A code of silence prevails. Through the plate glass store window I saw the proprietor rake gnarled fingers through close cropped hair as he talked to a customer who was no farmer.

The man I was searching for left the store carrying a bag of groceries and walked to my car. I cranked down my window. As he leaned over to talk the open V of his shirt revealed a triangle of sun-tanned skin. Farmer or not, this man worked the fields. "Heard you're asking 'bout me, he said."

"Yes, major."

His face tightened into a frown. "Can't say I'm happy you're here."

"I have a few questions."

"I've answered all of them years ago." His lips pressed together. A tight slash of anger.

"I've read your deposition, Major."

He stepped to his truck, turned and said: "Following me home is trespassing, you know."

I nodded at the Winchester racked in the window

behind the driver's seat. "I know about trespassing."

"Then you understand me." He set the groceries in his cab and turned to the store. "No one here says a bad word 'bout me."

"I'm not trying to open old wounds, Major."

He climbed into the pick-up. "You had your day in court so why don't you leave us be?"

"There's not going to be another trial."

He stared through his open window. "Then why not leave good enough alone?"

"I want to understand how it happened."

His fist tightened on the steering wheel. Gnarled knuckles whitening. "Books been written. Not a one got it right. Not a one."

"I know."

He laughed. "Well, maybe I can help you," he said, face flushed, a hand chopping air. Unsmiling gun-metal eyes fixed on mine. "People were frightened. Respectable people got paranoid fever. In Ohio you don't mock patriotism, you know."

He waited-out my silence. "Burning down the ROTC crossed a line. Students out of control." He hesitated. "Is that what you need to grab readers and get rich?"

"No."

"Well you can't raise the dead with a book. The families accepted the compensation money so what's there to write about?"

"How it happened."

"No one knows. Killing was an aberration for the Guardsmen. As their Chaplain I knew every one of them. The only deadly threat was giving M1's to week-end warriors who puked their guts out when they saw they killed someone. Yes. There was remorse. And

God knows what else. My job was to help soldiers deal with what they felt. And I guess I failed. But no matter what you write these troopers are my boys, every one of them, and when I call them son I mean it."

THIRTY TWO

"Love bears all things," intoned Reverend Billy his voice audible to the last row of mourners. "Love believes all things," he said, nodding at the casket poised over an open grave. His voice breaking he cried: "Love bears all things, and, above all, in life, as in death, love endures."

Our President agreed. His wife's favorite song counterpointed the eulogy. The lyrics "Ya gotta have heart!" evoked her smile, laughter, and unforgettable courage. Yes, how she loved that song. "Ya gotta have heart!"

"Above all," Reverend Billy said, his voice resonating: "A noble wife and mother was blessed with no longer fashionable virtues. Character. Loyalty. Courage."

Our President wanted to shout: Yes! She never had it easy. Never. Not like those who had it easy. And yes, she never complained. Never. Our President lifted his eyes to gaze at the blue smog-free sky recalling how she thought him mad when first they met. And she was right. So right. Mad to propose after knowing her three hours. Mad in love. Two years a-courting to persuade her to say yes.

And please Reverend Billy, remember Panama. Talk about her visits to Panama. Tell about the lepers; the love they felt when she embraced untouchables. Caressed disfigured faces. Held fingerless hands. Don't forget Panama. Like Jesus. She really cared for lepers.

Our President closed his eyes as the casket descended into the grave. A beautiful lady in a plain cloth coat was no more and yes, she deserved a better man. But don't mention that Reverend Billy. Not today. Not today. Talk about how she said we lived the American dream even after it became a horror show.

THIRTY THREE

The hospice of the Sisters of Saint Jude was a gray fieldstone building on a high granite bluff overlooking a broad river valley. There, at reception, a nursing sister in a starched white habit issued my visitors pass. On the walls of the corridor leading away from her desk rows of lights memorialized deceased residents with small bulbs attached to bronze name plates.

Twinkling walls of memory.

In a half-lit room on the third floor the Prosecutor lay connected to a spider web of IV catheters dripping vital fluids into his veins. On the wall above his bed a luminescent oscilloscope traced the dance of life timed to the pinging and blinking of a heart monitor.

His familiar grin welcomed me.

"You read my letter?"

"Yes sir."

"Strictly off-record. A backgrounder."

"Yes sir."

He lowered his gaze to fathom a thought. "No one's ever interviewed me before."

"Your name's not in the transcripts."

Unsurprised, he lifted his eyes. "Is that why

you're here?"

"Your name's conspicuous by its absence, sir."

He heard and smiled. Shaking his head. "That's a laugh," he said. "My fifteen minutes of fame. Or should I say shame?"

"Not shame, sir."

"Death-bed confessions are good for the soul my Jezzie teachers said." His chin trembled. He paused to watch my recorder blink each word. Then, closing his eyes, he nodded to the beeping of the heart monitor. "You ask how did we conceal the identity of the most active troublemakers? We had a hundred photographs. Took only three days to make a list. Everyone knows it's illegal to disclose Grand Jury names but we were told it's sometimes necessary to obstruct justice to serve justice. And I went along with that sophistry. Telexed the list to Washington where the most provocative demonstrators were deleted from the indictment."

He descended into memory. Into remorse. "An obstruction of justice is not easy to live with, you know." He nodded at each monitor beep. "The truth is I did what I was asked knowing damn well it was illegal." He stared at the blinking recorder light. "Hurts like hell when confession does nothing for you. As the Jezzie's say I leaped into a moral abyss with both eyes open and then despised what I had done. What I had become. What I am now. Because I'm not like the bastards I listened to. No way. Going along with their lies. Not like them. No. Never."

He lowered his eyes to stare at the catheters plugged into his forearm. The life-sustaining flow seemed an unacceptable intrusion. A violation of dignity. He looked up, eyes fixed on mine and suppressed a laugh. "Don't know why they're keeping me alive. I signed a

DNR. A Do Not Resuscitate order and still they will not pull the plug. They refuse to understand I had my one big moment, the one great moral challenge on which my whole life turned and all I thought about was protecting my career."

I switched-off the recorder and turned away finding little pleasure in another man's shame. The Prosecutor reached out and grasped my hand. "I know my dirty little secret is hard to listen to. My mistake. My bad judgment. Backing down when I had a chance to do what was right knowing the pencil of God has no eraser. So you tell me - is a dishonored life worth living?"

THIRTY FOUR

"Ha! Ha!
Where's your Pa?
He's in the White House
Ha! Ha! Ha!

Recalling a bawdy campaign verse Our President thought about president Cleveland's mistress, estranged wife, and illegitimate child who never thwarted his career. Hoover, Grant, and the Johnsons endured a bad press. Taylor, Harrison and FDR had fatal illnesses; Lincoln, Garfield, McKinley and JFK were assassinated.

Yes indeed, presidents endure vicious satiric verse, and crowds chanting:

I smell chicken
I smell ham,
I smell Herbert Hoover
In the garbage can!"

And what about that most despicable political slogan: "Don't let a cripple cripple the country"?

Well, you can rely on presidential funerals being historic. Always. Lincoln's train draped in black traveling to Springfield. Mourners crowding the rails.

FDR's casket carried down Pennsylvania avenue on a horse-drawn cassion. Bobby Kennedy's last journey delayed by mourners blocking the tracks. And who can forget VIP's slow-marching past John John saluting his daddy's casket? Mourning crowds waiting in the rain. Muffled drums. Fallen glory.

On a yellow pad, each word underlined, Our President wrote: Forget about a cross-country funeral train. What if nobody comes? And many of my friends will vanish with the shifting political winds. Update the names of my pallbearers. On my stone please inscribe:

> "I have done the best
> for my country"

THIRTY FIVE

At the Westwood nursing home residents did not fall. No fractured hips, broken legs, or concussions threatened seniors traveling down hallways in wheel chairs. "Let them have wheels!" a geriatric specialist prescribed and so propelled by hand with no fear of injury the aged and infirm rolled on into their twilight years. Occasionally some patients abandoned their wheelchairs to attempt a few tottering steps stabilized by aluminum frames. An effort restricted to patients denied heavy sedation.

On the nursing home walls photographs, cards, and children's drawings kept alive fading images of family identity. Above The Old Soldier's bed only a tattered regimental pennant bespoke a past of honorable service to our country. Not one picture of family or friends memorialized his personal life. Slumped in a chair, wrapped in a blanket, the Old Soldier dozed in a beam of sunlight streaming through a window.

Close-trimmed white hair and a commanding presence proclaimed once a soldier. Always a soldier. Now fading away.

I explained my visit.

"Did you bring cigars?" he demanded.

"No sir."

He turned from the window, backlit. Face in shadow. "Without a decent cigar," he said. "I don't think I have anything to say."

"With emphysema smoking's not allowed, sir."

A rattling wheeze confirmed my diagnosis. His voice cracked. "Shouldn't stop a clever young man like you." He grinned, straining for breath. "Enemies in high places, you know. Important enemies. No cigar is punishment for my crimes." Squeezing the inhaler to suck in air, he moved away from the window, turning in his chair to look at me. Eyes narrowed. A commanding stare. "Don't believe me, do you?"

"Yes sir."

"Even a paranoid can have real enemies."

"You're not paranoid, sir."

He nodded. Laughed. "They said mine was a fine Italian hand, you know. A Wop in Ohio can never be a 'Good Old Boy.' Just a whistle-blower who couldn't go along with lies."

"I know all about that, sir."

"Told the truth to the Grand Jury. The FBI. The presidential commission."

"I've read the transcripts."

"Testified sixteen times."

"Yes sir."

"Inadmissible evidence the judge ruled after I said my men had no reason to open fire."

He struggled for breath. Lips pursed. Cheeks ballooned to clear swollen bronchi. Lungs refilling through narrowed airways.

"Only students were indicted," he said. "Victims

judged to be law-breakers. They said one girl was pregnant and filthy. The boys high on drugs. Lies. All lies."

He slumped in his chair squeezing the inhaler. "People do terrible things you know. Like when my parents came to Ohio everyone was terrified of Reds, Blacks and Catholics."

The nurse in the doorway tapped one finger on her wristwatch. Time to go.

The Old Soldier held my arm. "Did you know the Klan's Grand Wizard told everyone the Pope's coming to Ohio?" He wheezed and coughed, strength ebbing. "Like what was said about hippies and communist revolutionaries coming here." His voice cracked. The nurse stepped to his chair. The Old Soldier smiled. Pleading. "Five minutes more, dear," he said. "Five minutes." Squeezing the inhaler she helped him take another deep breath. His grip tightened on my arm. "I knew what was going to happen."

The nurse rolled the wheelchair to his bed. The Old Soldier protested. "I haven't told how Klansmen gathered at the train stations waiting for the Pope."

The nurse suppressed a laugh. Again the inhaler restored his trembling voice. "On the radio the Grand Wizard said the Pope always traveled disguised. Our mayor had a telegram with the arrival time of the Pope's train and everyone went down to the station on foot, in model T's, on horses, in buggies, driving mules that could just about pull a wagon. At the depot the crowd was larger than when Harding spoke about "Back to Normalcy." Why they even had a big wooden cross for burning with tar and feathers and a greased pole to ride the Pope back across the state line. Some Klansmen had horse whips and ropes for a real old time KKK reception. And when that train chugged into the station, whistle blowing, bell clanging, the shouting and screaming could be heard clear across the state of Ohio."

The Old Soldier raised his hand. The nurse stepped back. Interested. She hadn't heard this story before.

"The only passenger on that train was a little fellow from back east in a black suit and vest wearing one of those dude derby hats Drummers are so fond of. For that's all he was, A salesman with a leather suitcase full of shoes. The crowd been duped by the Klan and the mayor. Which was why everyone insisted this little man just had to be the Pope. People had to believe the long arm of Satan had come to Ohio only no one could explain his suitcase filled with shoes. The salesman showed an order pad with Morton Shoe Company printed on top each page and he swore he was not the Pope even though he was wearing a black suit. And then they discovered he wasn't even Catholic.

Well, it was only the sheriff kept the crowd from lynching that mayor when they saw the telegram had no train number or arrival time or one word about the Pope. It was only the sheriff saved that mayor from the mob. Which just goes to show you what kind of citizens we have in our beautiful state of Ohio."

THIRTY SIX

Saved from darkness and obscurity by fragments of memory I learned the will to live outlasts everything but death. I struggled against being dissolved in a universal confusion knowing nothing, loving nothing. With unclouded eyes and relentless anger I refused to accept a vacuous life. My dreams, imaginings, and apparitions connected me to the past and through them the fabulous appeared.

Driving through a landscape of fashionable homes bordering a tree-lined highway I sought evidence only our reclusive ex-President could provide. For several miles my mirror revealed a police car turning with me at each intersection. I checked my speedometer. Used only proper turn signals. Obeyed all stop signs. Yet a sense of breaking a law prevailed. I pulled to the curb to study a roadmap. A State Trooper parked behind me and walked to my window. With a smile and a reassuring nod he removed mirrored sun glasses and leaned over to request my license and registration.

"Please get out of your car," he ordered.

Without hesitation I stepped onto the pavement.

"Put your hands on the roof."

Tutored by television I complied.

He patted down my legs and sides retrieving a tape recorder from my pocket.

"I'm a lawyer," I explained, arms dropping to my side. "I interview people."

He opened the recorder. Examined the interior. Satisfied, he handed it to me and nodded. "Open your trunk, please."

I turned the key. Up popped the lid. He peered inside. "Your spare needs air," he said, nodding at the tire. "There's a service station at the next traffic light," he explained, eyes again hidden behind opaque sun glasses. With a courteous sweep of his arm he waved me on.

"Sorry to stop you," he said. "This area's high-security you know."

I agreed. Even an ex-President deserves protection.

I drove on following a black-topped county road bordered by handsome "I have made it" estates. After four winding miles past the intersection a line of parked cars narrowed the highway with only one lane open for traffic. Another courteous trooper waved me past what I recognized as Our President's home.

The lights were on in the evening twilight. On the lawn, masked figures in Halloween costumes gathered at the front door. Gorillas and Pirates and "Masters of the Universe" holding "Trick or Treat" bags surrounded Our President who majestically strolled among delighted children as a bountiful king distributing packages of candy, laughing and smiling sharing their exuberant joy.

At one side of the lawn, in a dazzling blaze of flashbulbs, parents photographed the event. Other spectators reached out to shake Our President's hand.

Three laughing celebrants wore masks of presidents Carter, Ford, and Kennedy greeting our delighted President who graciously posed embracing his predecessors' surrogates.

As I intended neither a Trick nor a Treat, I drove away from this holiday scene hoping to try my investigative luck another day.

THIRTY SEVEN

"How involved were you?" I asked, turning on my recorder. The Student Organizer froze, eyes narrowing as he stared at the blinking red light. After thirty years habitual suspicions still surfaced. Self-discipline evoked haunting fears: Who was I working for? FBI? CIA? His body language proclaimed even a paranoid has real enemies. I remained silent as he shrugged and laughed, his unspoken answer - what the hell - I'm history. My jail time's something I honor.

"I was one hundred per cent involved," he said proudly, no longer reluctant. "I felt we were on the verge of something that was growing. And then Kent State happened and we said everyone go to Washington and make this the most militant demonstration ever."

Tall, thin, laconic, graying hair above a youthful honest face like Jimmy Stewart's Mr. Deeds. Or was it Mr. Smith who went to Washington? Despite years of teaching, speaking no longer came easy. The brilliant flow of words that enlightened classrooms was now hesitant. Controlled.

"Every night Walter Cronkite came on TV with a map and blinking lights showing the number and locations of campus demonstrations had increased to more than five hundred so we expected tomorrow's protest would be the apocalypse. I even wrote out my will."

He paused, shrugged and continued with a smile. "The next day I walked to the ellipse and saw people sunning themselves. Throwing Frisbees. Wading nude in the tidal basin. I said what's going on? What's happening? Where's the demonstration? Where's the militancy? Then someone yelled: 'We got a Tank! We took a Tank!' and I ran towards them thinking Right On! Now we really are in business!"

A painful image brushed away his smile. Eyes fixed on mine as he looked into the past.

"Well, it was only a group of Flower Children sitting on a tank sunning themselves, smoking pot with a soldier so I thought 'It's over. Whatever we were building is now over.'"

Silence. I sat motionless not wanting to interrupt his reverie, waiting for him to compose himself. It was as if he was alone. Recalling futility.

"And that's when we went downhill as a movement that had some chance of becoming potent. Kent State was the watershed. A surprise. A "Choke Point" where we came up to and faced reality and backed away. We did not cross that line because we saw demonstrations could be like what's going on in Vietnam... killing. You know. Real serious shit. And we weren't ready for it."

He shook his head. Staring at the recorder as if seeking a solution to unanswerable questions.

"That line was not crossed by militant whites. That line was not crossed by nationalist blacks. That line was not crossed by liberals. Only the government crossed that line into violence."

He rose from his chair pacing back and forth. A teacher, outlining his thoughts on a blackboard.

"Young people today are cynical because they have nothing to believe in. I had the United States to believe in. I had the Constitution to believe in and when I saw what was happening I said this is not right. We have to fix the things in our country that are broken."

"And so you began organizing demonstrations?"

"Yes. Demonstrations were how we built confidence that we were in control of our lives. We weren't just being confrontational. Militant. We were showing we were different... we had power... and we knew how to exercise that power. Not in ways that would hurt people but in ways saying we can take control. We can run our lives and don't want to be what our parents want us to be. Our Mantra was: 'All power to the imagination!'"

"And what do you regret?"

"Some things couldn't be helped. By 1970 we couldn't keep track of all the dissenters coming into the movement. Middle class kids some from elite schools would come to meetings and two weeks later they would set something on fire and go to jail for ten years. They were so quickly swept up in the emotions we evoked, that we created, they made commitments they really didn't understand."

THIRTY EIGHT

"This is my letter to the world that never wrote to me" said a poet in despair at ever receiving a reply to her questions. And so it was with my futile effort to elicit answers from Our ex-President. My quest for truth evoked more suspicion than facts. Letters to a sad old man reopened unhealed wounds. My name appeared on the FBI "Watch List." A potential threat. Life never was the same.

Two Secret Service agents visited me. Young. Polite. Dark suits. White shirts. Conservative neckties. Never raised their voices. Were they vetting me for a Justice Department job I wondered? But no. Their message was clear. Stop writing disturbing letters to Our ex-President.

I quoted Thomas Jefferson - "We have Petitioned for redress in the most humble terms: Our repeated petitions have been answered by repeated injury."

Steel-eyed stares. A response reserved for "Fruitcakes" and "Crazies" stalking presidents. The agents didn't recognize my reply was published July 4th, 1776 at Independence Hall, Philadelphia. If psychological profiles are what they think with, what use is history? They agreed I demonstrated no potential for violence. However my letters justified inclusion in a presidential threat database.

Today a database and ubiquitous surveillance cameras are watching over me. Over all of us. Watching and recording. Without permission. Anonymous eyes now scrutinize my God-given identity and learn more details of my life than I can possibly remember. A database never forgets. Memory banks are as eternal as the Pyramids. From cradle to the grave we are watched and recorded and intimidated. To what end?

Liberty and Privacy, Freedom's foundation are so entangled, that surrendering one, you lose the other too. Our language becomes televised chatter, the true meaning of words abandoned. Our unanswered questions do great harm. For no man can re-shape the narrative of events that is his life no matter how many exculpatory books he publishes. No matter how much we try to conceal troubling facts and events, memory remains. History can not be deceived and it is impossible to hide the truth forever.

THIRTY NINE

A Student Activist, now a tenured professor near retirement, agreed to be interviewed at home. The oak-paneled walls of his study displayed photographs of demonstrations he had led. On a coffee table beside my recorder a framed cover of TIME pictured him storming the ramparts of the Pentagon waving an anti-war banner.

The years had softened his thin intense face. Gray tufts of hair framed a prominent forehead. He seemed eager to recall the most exciting moments of his life. As he spoke in precise outbursts of words his eyes grew larger, his voice sharper. "I think there is a sense of decency in this country that was born in the sixties and is still with us today," he said.

He rose from his chair and walked to the kitchen. In a moment he returned with two Pepsi cans. Pulling the tabs he offered one to me.

"Is the recorder still on?" he asked. I looked at the tumbling numbers in the footage counter and nodded.

He sat at the coffee table and grinned. "Whenever I travel and meet veterans of the sit-ins and demonstrations I find a sense of recognition binds us however much we have grown apart. After all, we were the sons and daughters if not of the ruling class but of something pretty close to it. We were children of the elite."

"I believe you led the first Collective."

He restrained a laugh. "Right," he said. "But collective action is not the sum total of individual wills. People become 'collective' accidentally. That is why 'play acting,' having fun, became so important. And I'm not talking about Woodstock. Woodstock was a parody of what we meant by freedom because freedom entails an affirmation of justice not simply removal of all restraints."

Again he rose and moved to the window to stare at the meadow behind his home. With his back turned to me he said: "I think we were naive about the nature of authority and I think we were naive about the importance of discipline in producing results."

"Is that why there was so much violence?"

"No," he replied. "What was violent was being forced to choose between our need for personal integrity and loyalty to our government. A choice no one should be compelled to make." He turned to me. Calm blanketed his face. Eyes fixed on mine. A thoughtful look. Only his lips moved. "Loyalty and not community is the basis of our society so we made disloyalty our creed."

Walking towards me, hands gesturing dramatically as he spoke, I sensed his persuasive power. "For us freedom from all bonds became our strategy. Alienation allowed us to act without being restrained by our professors or institutions. Our first demonstrations were peaceful because it had not occurred to us that once we presented the contradictions of their position to those who were running the country they would see the light and recognize us who after all we were their children."

Suddenly excited he stepped to the window. He invited me to stand beside him. A family of deer grazed in the backyard. Enthralled, he could not conceal child-like joy. "Now that's a happening," he said, happily. "A natural event. Not like a demonstration." We remained at the window until a barking dog frightened the deer away.

"What Vietnam did was not only change our consciousness but also change the consciousness of the country. We believed we were on a collision course with our parents generation bringing a different world into being than the world they hoped we would accept and live in. In the anti-war movement our response to every reply when we were demanding the impossible was: "Let's see. Let's test the waters.""

I interrupted to insert a fresh cassette into the recorder.

He could hardly wait to continue.

"It was an experimental time and our experiments took the form of self-destructiveness in drugs and sexuality. Political change was tested with our bodies, minds, and imaginations to see whether or not what people told us was impossible was in fact possible. Most of the time they were right. Some of the time, they were wrong. And when they were wrong, and what we hoped to happen actually did happen we gained confidence in our ability to make the world a better place."

He went to the kitchen and returned with a knife, a loaf of bread, a jar of guava jelly and two bottles of Poland Springs water. "I baked this myself," he said, laughing. "Eat right, drink right and you'll live forever." He cut the bread covering two slices with guava.

"Did we succeed?" He paused to hand me a slice. "I don't think this kind of effort is ever over. I think with sit-ins and mass demonstrations we experienced more human connections. I think we acquired a passion for not only justice but also an intense kind of camaraderie, a sister and brotherhood that stayed with us. A profound kind of feeling.

"And what remains of that feeling?"

"If anything has been lost it is not the politics or the vision so much as it is the sense of what it takes to make real friendship possible. And by real friendship I don't mean simply two people sharing with each other the aches and pains of the aging process. I mean people who dream of a better world they want to build with a sense of moving through life together and wanting to help the other person be there with you. That kind of friendship. That kind of love."

"And you still believe that?"

"Many of the things I advocated thirty years ago I would not advocate today. I have become more sophisticated and I hope more realistic about what is possible and what isn't. I think the sixties were a great time. And yes a lot of people were hurt because the sacrifices they made were never rewarded. Some never acquired a sense of trust and caring and tried to fill their emptiness with drugs and other things that made them feel they had a center in their being for at least the moment they were high on drugs or were having sex and I think that ultimately a lot of them suffered a great deal."

"How do you explain this to students today?"

"I tell them the sixties must be understood like the depression years. We rejected success. We rejected the suburbs. We were alienated from the conventional symbols of success and I think the final question is what did we make of our alienation?"

"What did you make of it?"

"We began talking to each other in a way that never happened before. The protests, confronting authorities, rejecting our teachers gave us a sense of equality and justice richly connected to the ideals of this country. And when they came in and broke our heads and put us in jail they did it because what we were doing scared them more than the actual threat of our protests."

He leaned forward and stared at the blinking red light. Assured the recorder was ON he paused to define his thoughts.

"I don't think anybody who went through these experiences is the same person that they would have been had they not had that experience. I think the shock on students faces at Kent State when the National Guard fired at them and the shock on the faces of the National Guard pulling the triggers was a realization that this confrontation was inevitable. What you see in those eyes is I want to reach out and make contact with you and it's not going to happen."

Then, his voice stronger, he said: "What we were saying is that there is another way of being with each other. And it is a better way. And that is what the sixties and seventies really were. A time that gave us a basis for looking critically at the rest of our lives."

As if embarrassed by his feelings he became professorial, subdued. "All of us benefited from that experience. Some still feel exiled. And in a way we all were. We had experienced a substantial dose of alienation. And the ability to use that alienation as a springboard for growing up, for becoming ourselves was what was unique about that time."

FORTY

Am I out of my mind imagining dangers that do not exist? I turn and look behind me whenever I go for a walk. I study reflections in store windows as I pass. I stop at street corners stepping into doorways to see if I am being followed.

Am I being followed? Or seeing shadows? Apparitions?

Yesterday a taxi drove past as I left my office, a Yellow Cab with no one in the back seat, moving a bit faster than my walk, maybe four miles an hour and I wondered why this late at night the driver didn't solicit me as a fare.

Perhaps he was reading numbers on office buildings, searching for a street address? But no, as I continued walking I turned and saw the driver wasn't looking at doorways but into his side view mirror, watching me. I slowed my pace. His red tail light flashed as he touched the brake pedal.

What exactly are they trying to find out?

I don't use my telephone. I know what a normal dial tone sounds like. No clicks, hums or buzzing static. Just the honest tone of privacy guaranteed by our Constitution. Now I share a "Party Line" with my government with no clue about who is taping my every word or why.

If they want to know what I think read my letters. Or watch student protests on TV. Following me, taping my conversations is expensive, time consuming and stupid.

Don't tell me they don't know exactly what students are doing. They know very well it's impossible to keep secrets from our government when they had so many informers demonstrating with us.

FEDERAL BUREAU OF INVESTIGATION
TO: The Director (CONFIDENTIAL)
FROM: GEL
SUBJECT: David Constant

Named subject observed from vehicle leaving office on foot at 22:00 hours at end of working day (10:00 hours to 18:00 hours usual) proceeded north on La Salle street to destination now unknown. Heavy traffic density at this time (red lights) resulted in loss of visual contact at 22:45 hours though named subject unaware of surveillance. Threat indication monitoring of telephone and telex negative. Visual contact lost at 22:45 hours resumed at 10:00 hours next morning.

FORTY ONE

He was our most ancient Professor Emeritus. Chair of the philosophy department. Disciple of Gandhi. Ordained minister and former "Freedom Rider" traveling through the blood-stained south to register voters. A distinguished scholar who believed if you are a first-class thinker your life and behavior should be a piece with your thought.

The blinking red eye of my tape recorder evoked a smile. "I've never lectured a machine before," he said, watching the revolving reels. "What an audience! A little black box that can't talk back."

We sat in an enclosed garden behind his home interrupted every ten minutes by the high-pitched roar of jets descending on final approach to a nearby airport. The intrusion was accepted without complaint. A fact of suburban life.

He insisted I submit my questions in advance. Intellectual certainty replaced hesitation without painfully groping the past. He knew what he wanted to say and though age had subdued his deep voice he spoke incisively. "You asked about the student bomber," he began. "Well, at first I thought he was just another immature activist... in no way unique except for his extra-curricular activity, rowing. He was from a fine catholic family. Very conservative."

"Like many of our most active radicals," I added.

He nodded. Raised his eyes skyward as if anticipating another thundering jet. "Yes. True," he said. "And if at first you only engage in symbolic protests, sit-ins, demonstrations and draft card burnings it's not difficult to take the next step and embrace the notion that the urge to destroy is a creative urge."

"A prevalent idea, I replied."

He smiled. Nodded agreement. "An idea that became a student mantra inspiring bombings not intended to be only symbolic but to do millions of dollars damage. A student activist thinks he's engaged in something inevitable... making history with no individual in control and that is what absolves him from responsibility for his actions. Students really wanted to instigate a revolution... lose themselves in something larger than themselves desperately believing in their fantasy."

"Which the media validated. Made real."

There was a long moment of silence before he continued. His voice tinged with regret. "The media blurred the distinction between reality and fantasy. Watching themselves on television students came to not only deny the truth of certain basic propositions of our society... they also denied the existence of truth and developed elaborate arguments to buttress their denial. Television helped students delude themselves about the mood of the country convinced they were creating a revolution and just a little push would make it happen. Demonstrations in Paris, Korea, Japan, and Mexico made it seem as if students were taking over the world when in fact the base of their movement was very narrow and they failed to lead the country into any profound changes. Then to everyone's surprise the violence ended. It was all over. The establishment's worst fears proved unfounded no matter what the pundits predicted."

I watched him for a moment. Reluctant to interrupt. To break the silence I asked: "How did it happen so suddenly?"

In a saddened voice he answered: "In October 1970 a student bank robbery killed a police officer in Boston. A shocking act and one of many that wrecked the student movement. Most students also resented the bomb scares that closed campuses. They sympathized with college administrators who were open to legitimate protest and tried to keep the universities going. Then the war was Vietnamized. The Lottery replaced the Draft. Students lost their fear of going to war. That's when the demonstrations ended."

"Leaving students empowered."

He nodded. Hesitating a moment before replying. "They had the nation's attention for several years and if you equate attention with power that would explain the intensity of their fantasies and the faculty's reaction to their illusion of power. As Voltaire observed watching a mob parade down a street: 'There goes the mob and I must follow them because I am their Leader'... Some faculty were trying to keep their leadership position by following the students... or by pretending to follow them."

He rose from his chair and turned away to ponder a disturbing memory.

"There was an erosion of respect for the faculty," he said, his voice suddenly energized. "We were no longer authority figures who had influence on students or at least believed we had. There was also a widespread disrespect for all other institutions. The faculty ceased to be persuasive role models."

FORTY TWO

I now take my daily walk in the evening to allow fading light to protect my anonymity. At this hour sidewalks are uncrowded, people are at home watching TV. Cars curbed for the night. I nod and smile at other pedestrians confidant I am not recognized. I greet a policeman as we pass. I nod. He touches his cap with a nightstick returning a friendly salute. A few paces behind I hear the tread of footsteps in step with my own. I slow down. Breathe deep. Relax. The footsteps come closer as a tall, long-legged fellow, about my age wearing a blue jogger's sweatsuit strides past. At the next intersection he turns right. I smile, dismiss my baseless fears, continue a steady, comfortable pace.

At the corner, waiting for the light to change, I glance into a store window reflecting the street behind me. Empty. Not a soul in sight. I relax. Enjoy the night air. Free of the confines of my apartment. The light turns green. I cross the street and step out on to the avenue. What a lovely evening.

Crowded. Noisy. Cars grinding gears. Horns honking. Much traffic. I walk half a block. Again, footsteps. Unmistakable footsteps pacing my own.

Should I slow down and see who is on my tail? Reveal I know I'm followed? Fear blurs thought. Coward that I am I continue walking. Pace unchanged. Confrontation avoided.

In the distance, waiting at the far corner, staring into a brightly lit store window, the jogger in the blue sweatsuit. I abruptly turn to watch my "Tail" step off the curb and stride across the street.

"Spooks" doing their job. Obeying orders of a somewhat hysterical president.

But considering my letters. What exactly do they have in mind for me? "Preventative Detention?"

FEDERAL BUREAU OF INVESTIGATION
TO: The Director (CONFIDENTIAL)
FROM: GEL
SUBJECT: David Constant

Observation of named subject reestablished this date. Resumed foot surveillance (avoiding traffic problem) at 22:35 hours. (note longer working day). Proceeding south on La Salle street away from place of employment. Named subject for reasons unknown walked in direction opposite from day previous. Named subject demonstrated awareness of surveillance confirmed by loss of visual contact at 23:15 hours. Threat indication monitoring of telephone and telex negative.

FORTY THREE

"Inadmissible Evidence" ruled the judge and so the Kent State dead died twice; once when they were killed and again when a judge exercising "Judicial Discretion" covered up the crime that killed four students. In the now blind eyes of the law what happened on Blanket Hill never happened. A decision applauded nationwide to our country's shame and my regret.

With "The Law" declining to bear witness finding reliable witnesses silenced by years of amnesia was no small achievement. A reluctance to speak of the past thwarted my search for truth. Letters of inquiry returned "Address Unknown." Phone calls were unanswered. Only our alumni magazine enabled me to locate survivors and penetrate a wall of stolid silence and denial. My frustration and despair lifted when working late one night I looked up from my desk and greeted an old professor of mine.

Popular. Generous with grades. A campus celebrity. He filled every seat in our largest auditorium lecturing on "Rebel Thought." With uncontained emotion he talked about Socrates, Galileo, Voltaire,

Swift, Tom Paine, Thoreau, and Gandhi. His voice quavering, students seated up front saw his handsome face flush with passion as he spoke. His trembling hands shuffling notes.

He never answered my request for an interview. And when I confronted him he explained his lawyers insistence on silence anticipating an indictment. When I turned on my tape recorder he welcomed this opportunity to revisit a past that was not without regret.

Eyes closed. Voice firm. Free to speak.

"No doubt we overestimated our influence and underestimated our responsibility. Students come to us for advice. You do your best and there's no way to judge the impact of what you say. There's a war going on and you're the adult, know all the answers, and students are confused. Searching. Troubled. At war with themselves, their parents. The government. Don't trust anyone over thirty was their mantra. And then you go to class one morning and it's an earthquake. Students stopped looking to us for leadership even though we were sympathetic. We never objected to peaceful demonstrations. We supported them until they showed no interest in rational persuasion. Their angry rhetoric alienated the administration and the town. Then, when they turned against us we knew we could not control students who didn't give a damn for what we thought. We were irrelevant observers. Spectators. Non-participants except for the twenty-three who signed a protest statement and were called subversives responsible for the tragedy their teaching made inevitable.

Several of us wearing the blue armbands of Faculty Marshals tried to disperse demonstrators. But only after four students were dead. All I can say on my behalf is that I did ask the General not to confront the students again. I pleaded with him to give the Marshals time to cool down their anger. But by then I had no credibility.

"They must learn what law and order is all about!" he replied, turning to his Adjutant. "Take this man away!" he ordered, pointing his swagger stick at me. "And, as you know, the rest is history."

FORTY FOUR

Last night, opening three burglar proof locks, I entered my apartment, walked through the foyer and switched on the light in the living room. I sat in my favorite arm chair, leaned back, but could not relax. I felt discomforted. Troubled. The paintings on the wall, the bookcases, sofa, coffee table, and desk seemed out of place. Different. I stepped into the bedroom and opened a bureau drawer. Passport, wristwatch, and cash box were untouched. Reassured I had not been robbed I went to the kitchen and turned on the stove. A glass of warm milk would welcome this tired traveler home.

In the living room the impression something was amiss persisted. I had been gone four days. Dust had accumulated. My cleaning lady had not worked her magic during my absence.

The kettle summoned me to the kitchen. Returning to the living room, milk glass in hand, I went to a bookcase to find a comforting book to read.

What I found did not set my mind at ease.

The bookcases covering the walls from floor to ceiling are my pride and joy. Shelved separately, rows of books, sectioned into fiction, non-fiction, and law are readily accessible. I can reach out and instantly find any book I want.

But not tonight.

My well-ordered bookshelves were disarranged. Books had been taken down, opened, and searched for God's knows what hidden documents or research notes, and then carelessly replaced.

If I had been raped, I could not have felt more violated. That the rapist is my government made the pain even more excruciating.

FEDERAL BUREAU OF INVESTIGATION
TO: The Director (CONFIDENTIAL)
FROM: GEL
SUBJECT: Authorized Entry

Undetected surreptitious entry (USE) of named subject David Constant's residence negative. Threat indication monitoring of telephone and telex negative.

FORTY FIVE

God damn "Spooks!" Last week they invited me to their office downtown for questioning. A voluntary appearance. No arrest, subpoenas or coercion. Just friendly questions. Like why am I so often seen in your neighborhood? Will I continue to write letters you never answer? Am I now a stalker? My "Psychological Profile" doesn't look good. Perhaps some "Preventative Detention" would be smart. For my protection as well as yours.

They escorted me to a "Holding Room" asked me to stay overnight. A few more questions in the morning and then I could go, with many thanks for my cooperative attitude.

When the door was locked I found myself in a small bedroom. Purple walls covered with fluorescent velveteen psychedelic posters glowed under a blue light hanging from the ceiling. Concealed behind thick drapes, plywood covered the windows. Double-nailed to the frame. Along one wall. A bed. In one corner a TV. And on a table in the middle of the room, a dinner tray with a fresh salad, a bowl of soup, and a thick end-cut of roast beef. An offer I could not refuse. Hours of questioning builds an appetite.

Well, a meal, an evening watching TV and a good night's sleep is not exactly Alcatraz. I had nothing to hide. Answering all questions certainly would demonstrate they had nothing to fear from me.

After dinner I turned on TV. Surfed a few channels and decided on "Dr. No", an old James Bond flick. The voices seemed distorted as I adjusted the tuner, twisted the antenna. The colors melted, running down the tube. The images suddenly inverted as if a mad projectionist had threaded the film backwards. The dialogue became shrill. Piercing voices. Picture and sound began pulsating, timed to my labored breathing. I held my breath. The images stabilized. I began to count slowly, exhaling as the picture receded and voices became distant.

I turned off the TV and stretched out on the bed. The purple walls closed in. I held my breath. Resumed counting. When I reached fifty I could breath again and everything was OK The walls stopped moving.

Uncontrolled trembling began. I pressed my hand against my chest until all motion stopped. I could not move my legs. Hot and cold flashes soaked my shirt. A chilling sweat. I felt I was dying. Perhaps dead. Then, darkness lifted. My arms and legs began thrashing, kicking off the sodden blanket. I was alive and then dead and then alive again, and again.

I rolled off the bed. Vomited. Removed my shirt to clean up the mess, wiping it back and forth, scrubbing under the bed and along the wall.

A "Spook" stood in the doorway looking at me unsurprised. "We're taking you to the Hospital, sir," he said politely. "We're going to pump you out and see what kind of shit you've been using."

I dragged myself to the bed. struggling for balance. Hot and cold flashes coursed thru my body in convulsive shivers.

"I don't do drugs," I insisted. "Never."

"Seems to me, sir," he said, "You're boxed right out of your mind. Yes sir. Right out of your firkin' mind."

FORTY SIX

To take mystery out of reality I had language. A net to capture beauty. Entrap wonder. And to evoke the emotional odds and ends of a lifetime, to recall my bedlam of memories I tried prayer knowing there is no safe conduct through this landscape. At best - I hoped for a cease-fire. Amnesty. Grace.

Awakening from LSD evoked a love affair with the world. The stream of my being found new pathways. I acquired an avid curiosity seeing what I had not seen before.

Concealed within Jeff's exuberant charm - a pervasive sorrow. Paglacci the clown became Hamlet when he ceased protesting long enough to reveal himself. Sprawled on Blanket Hill watching clouds sail by, Jeff turned to look at me.

"Did you ever wonder what not knowing who you are is like?" he said.

A weird question. "Where are you coming from?" I asked.

At the foot of Blanket Hill our Victory Bell tolled. Students changing classes emerged from buildings to crowd walkways. Jeff reached out as if to grasp something elusive.

"Think about it," he said. "What if we had no past? What if everything we ever did, thought, or imagined vanished from our minds? No childhood memories. No nothing. How could we know who we are?"

I turned and looked at him. Hard. "What's with you?" I said. Puzzled.

Jeff ignored me. Shrugged. A cloud covered the sun. Rumbling high overhead a contrail traced a line of ice crystals across the sky. Jeff frowned. Retrieved a thought. Looked grim. "Losing your memory is worse than dying," he said. "With no memory death is a mercy."

"If you say so."

"We are nothing without our memory." Jeff said. Eyes fixed on mine. Troubled eyes. I refused to return his stare.

"Depends on who you think you are." I said, reassuring him. Dissatisfied, Jeff looked even more grim.

"Not remembering is worse than death."

I turned and studied my friend. Jeff lay on the grass, palms under his head looking up at the clouds. A most unhappy Troubadour.

"Can't take one moment in time and say that's who you are," I insisted. "We're continually changing."

"Tell me about it," Jeff said, smiling. "Grow a beard and you become someone else." As an image clouded his mind he said, "Wear long hair and you're a freak. Act a bit weird and they'll stick electrodes on your brain. Zap your memory away." He nodded. His face hardened. "Dreamt they stuck me in a tub of cold water with a rubber collar 'round my neck."

Taken aback, I stared at Jeff. Saw his fear. "That's

one hell of a nightmare," I said.

"There's no law against what shrinks can do when they claim you're crazy. No way you can stop them."

"How about cutting your hair? Shaving your beard?"

Jeff paused. Grinned. Then, remembering: "Once was tight with this guy back home who did a lot of drugs. Parents paid a thousand dollars a week to send him to shrinks to be cured."

"Of what?" I asked.

"Of being fifteen. Of doing dumb things. So he goes into convulsions during electro-shock and now doesn't do drugs or anything else 'cause he's dead. His parents' problem been solved. If you ask me he wasn't the one who was crazy."

"Should have run away from home."

"Damn right," Jeff said as he turned away and reached out as if to touch something unseen. "You know, I think if I couldn't make music I'd lose my mind. Seems like the whole world's gone mad."

"It has."

Silent. Searching for words, he shook his head. My blood ran cold. "Could happen," he said. "All these wars. The Bomb. A nut in the White House talking to paintings on the wall."

"Well, what do you expect from Our President?"

Visibly disturbed he stared at me for a moment, his eyes refusing to meet mine. "I sometimes see myself tied down in a hospital bed," he said. "My brain's burned out. I'm in a coma. I remember nothing."

"A bad dream."

"I'd rather be shot."

FORTY SEVEN

You might say I've paid my dues. In full. More than met the cost of being myself. Years of silence brought doubt and darkness. The exorbitant price of what little I've learned. As a foolish lover I've quarreled with the world and sleepless mocking nights alone intrude on the vastness of my memories. Matching wits with words, I struggle to find the truth revealed at the end of each sentence where a well-placed period drives an arrow into my all too human heart.

Never wore a prophet's cloak. Only "A Rememberer." A man lost in the confusion of knowing little, loving much.

"Talk is cheap," Will said, "an evasion, a cop-out." And I agreed. For me, writing is thinking. And the agony of not writing far exceeds the agony of laying down words, sentence by sentence. Long lines of words parading through my mind. Unstoppable as an avalanche.

"You all talk too much," Will said, interrupting my thought, flashing a boyish All-American grin. Friendly. Never hostile. "Consider what you are shouting."

"We have."

Will wore his ROTC uniform today as he walked with me to our next class. Unfazed by stares and anti-war graffiti scrawled on walls he stayed cool. Walked tall. Proud. He smiled and remained silent when someone called after him - "Napalming 105" or shouted - "Baby Killing 101." Fools. Not to be tolerated gladly.

"You don't need to listen to this," I said. "Why don't you get out of uniform at the Drill Hall?"

"Didn't have time to change. Besides, it's fun stirring up the animals."

Classmates walking ahead of us turned and stared. We were a mismatched pair. A remarkable sight on a campus where ROTC candidates kept themselves apart. Since Vietnam, that is.

"You could get hurt. There's some real crazies here."

Will reached up and closed the top button of his uniform. He smiled when I shook my head at such fidelity to the military dress code. Blanket Hill was no parade ground.

"Crazy talk is inflammatory," Will said. "Like torching the ROTC building. Or the president's house. Believing these threats is dangerous."

The bell at the foot of the hill tolled the hour. Walkways filled with students changing classes.

"Our business here is learning. Not demonstrating. Politics is not education," Will said.

"Where have you been?" I demanded. "There's a war on and we're invited and some of us don't want to go."

"And some of us waited a long time to get here. Worked and saved and sweated scholarships. What about us?"

I said nothing. What could I say? Close down the

school and some students don't get what they paid for.

"I'm the first in my family to go to college," Will said. "I've got aunts and uncles and cousins and grandparents and a mother counting days 'til graduation. Try and understand what graduation means to them. The country they fled they remember for cruelty and poverty and no hope to educate children for a life of more than hardship and hunger. A life without culture. Nyet Kulturyni my grandparents said. Nyet Kulturyni. Without culture. That's why my family can not understand students closing universities. Demonstrating. Striking. Burning College buildings. Trashing libraries. Holding hostage professors devoted to teaching what it is to be alive in mind and soul."

Will stopped in the doorway and turned to face me. Always a listener not a talker. Long speeches rare. He needed an answer. A good one.

I gave him my best off-the-pseudo-intellectual shelf reply. "Students are not just pissed-off in the good old U.S. of A. Students are tearing up streets in Paris. Mexico City. Tokyo. Students have had it. World-wide."

"Had what?" He leaned into me. Blocking the doorway. I could not step past him into the classroom.

I lowered my voice. Spoke slowly. Looked him in the eye. "Enough of the bullshit. The lies. Crap like 'Bombs for peace' or 'Better dead than red' or 'Destroying a village to save it.' You know, the Cold War bit."

Will laughed. Shook his head. "You're talking propaganda. Politics. Not education."

I raised my voice. Angry. Students turned in their

seats to listen. "I'm talking about what's on TV every night. The deceptions. The evasions. The half-truths. The smiling bloated talking heads justifying horror."

The class nodded agreement. An outcast in uniform, Will didn't give a damn who heard what he had to say.

"Going from campus to campus demonstrating is like burning down the house we live in. Must live in together. Left. Right. Rich. Poor. Black. White. Then, after everything of value's been torn down, dismissed, denigrated, you guys will finally stop and ask yourselves - where you're going to sleep tonight. And who you're going to live with, tomorrow."

FORTY EIGHT

At six o'clock in the evening as daylight fades over the rooftops of our troubled city I am bereft. A somber grey shroud covers the sky. A reluctant sunset abandons the horizon. In the street below my window flickering lights ward off muggings and other dangers, imagined or real. And yes, hopefully, tomorrow will bring another day of joy and sorrow, and the promise of love.

A chill wind wafts stagnant river odors up to my apartment and I close windows to ward off another revolting assault on my sense of well being. A high-pitched siren adds another grating voice to my vision of spreading urban decay and I wonder: Police? Fire Engine? Or EMT?

Seated in the dark, ignoring my TV, I listen to the sexual groaning of an elevator rising in the shaft on the far side of my living room wall. In the apartment overhead an out-of-tune piano runs through practice scales as a blaring radio down the hall shares today's catastrophic news with neighbors.

One advantage of living alone is solitude, a mirror in which to see others with sighted eyes and a feeling heart. And reluctantly, I also discover myself and what appears is not always admirable. What can I say about someone who is insensitive, distant and unpopular with classmates more concerned with having a good time?

On some evenings, surrendering to nostalgia, I see myself on Blanket Hill watching beautiful long-legged girls in cut-down shorts and T-shirts perfume the air with inviting laughter. My smug indifference is a wonderment today. Yes, I rationalized, I had more important matters on my mind than dating. More concerned with war and peace, the environment and civil rights than in getting laid. And that's the truth, dammit.

You see, after 1968 I was old before my time. Angry. Disappointed. Confused. In need of a cause worth fighting for.

Thirty years later, looking back, I recognize that something died in America in 1968. Hope. Optimism. A sense of possibility of what our country could be. For an outrageous children's army of student dissenters a certain kind of bittersweet idealism ended. 1968 was a dark year casting a tragic shadow over our lives. Assassinations aborted everything we had been fighting for, dividing a nation. The despised spokesmen of the past were back in the saddle appealing not to the nobler side of our fellow citizens but to their dark turbulent side. Fear. Prejudice. Hatred. The air was poisoned with messages of them against us, long-hairs against short-hairs, minorities against whites. Indeed our hope and dream that our country could heal itself died. Trashed was our belief and trust in government, church and family. And then, on May 4th 1970, what remained of our childlike innocence died at Kent

State and we knew we would never be young again.
Never.

FORTY NINE

Sometimes I am a mirror walking down the road that is my life. I look at myself dismayed at what I recognize as the high cost of reflection. Pain as a condition of existence. Doubt and confusion as the cost of learning to accept every consequence of living. To love knowing there is no easy return of love humbles the soul. And to know, to understand, becomes a passion. An addiction. And perhaps madness recalling names and faces across lonely years, through remembered unlived years, hearing only an echo of my own heart's tears.

Loneliness is every man's portion. Good men in a bad world change from good to bad and from bad to good, back and forth all their lives fighting death until at last they lose that fight always knowing they would.

"Not to see one's evil," said Allison interrupting my thoughts, "That is power. Unlimited power. Power accompanied by a self-righteousness that kills conscience." She turned on her side sipping coffee from a styrofoam cup. Sprawled on my back on an adjacent cot I looked up at the ceiling enduring a compulsory half hour of rest. Having someone to talk to at the Red Cross bank precluded boredom. We never donated alone. For twenty dollars we regularly gave a pint of blood. A transfusion that paid for meals for more than a week.

Along one wall of the clinic a row of army cots provided some comfort to donors after being punctured. The blue-gray fluorescent lights gave our faces a cadaverous pallor. I watched a nurse lay out a line of cotton swabs and needles. She turned and smiled as I declined a chocolate chip cookie. "How much longer?" I asked.

She glanced at her watch. "Ten minutes," she said, holding an empty cup. "More coffee? Orange Juice?"

"Coffee, please."

She handed me the cup. A small cup. No more than a swallow.

I grimaced at such frugality. Allison laughed. "Caffeine raises blood pressure," she said. "They don't want you to bleed to death."

"And the cookies?."

"Rocks. From a factory outlet. Three days old."

"Ask not what your country can do for you. Ask only what you can do for your country."

Allison grinned. "Don't be cynical. You take the money and hopefully save a G.I.'s life. Maybe you'll save more than one life. That's nothing to joke about."

"You're the joke, Allison. You protest the war and then give blood for reasons you insist are patriotic. Me, I'm honest. I'm here because I like to eat and twenty bucks buys a lot of food."

"I'm against unnecessary dying."

"Like what?"

"Like epidemics, prison riots, drug overdoses, the despair of urban ghettos, neglected seniors in nursing homes, kids killed in drive-by shootings, political dissenters murdered by death squads, civilians poisoned by nerve gases or toxic bacteria or radiation, or burned in fires, drowned in floods, buried in earthquakes, asphyxiated by killer-smogs, or dying from contaminated water, or from a speck of botulism in a hamburger."

"What about railway and airline disasters?" I asked.

The nurse interrupted to hand us an envelope containing money and a certificate of appreciation. "Thank you," she said. "You can go now."

I stood up. Unsteady on my feet. In a moment, fighting vertigo, I followed Allison to the street. Never affected by visits to the clinic she walked out of the building unfazed. An eternal fountain of blood.

We returned to our dorm without a word. I felt her anger. Really bad vibes.

"God damn it to hell," she said. "Why can't we ever talk?"

"You were talking. I was listening."

"You piss me off. You know that?"

"And you're a Johnny-one-note. Spouting the same song. Over and over. The same ideas. The same bullshit."

"Like what?"

"Like believing people can stop killing each other."

Allison halted and turned to block my path. She nodded. Her tolerant smile left no doubt her reply should be obvious if I had half a brain. "Well," she said, with a slight hesitation between words, "maybe donating a little blood now and then will save a few lives."

I didn't hesitate. Struck back. Hard. "Millions are dying and all you can think of is giving a pint of blood?"

Pained. Her eyes narrowed. A usual response when confronted by intractable obtuseness. "Right," she said now lecturing a cretin. "Save one life and you save the world."

"Your arithmetic is a fantasy. A bed-time story for children."

After a pause Allison shrugged her shoulders, clearly exasperated.

"Maybe. But it's a story that's visible. Look and you will see how one death results in other casualties. There are always shock waves. Reverberations. Echoes. Look and you will see that families are devastated when one member dies. Sorrow's signature is indelible. You have to live with some deaths forever."

Her voice breaking Allison turned and without a word hurried off ending the discussion. I did not follow. Stood there perplexed with egg on my face watching her long-legged arm swinging strides across campus. Many of her mysteries were untouchable. Off-limits. Out of bounds and respecting Allison's unknowns had certain rewards. Delight in the unexpected. The charm of surprises. Following the twists and turns of her uncommon mind I never knew what's coming next and no doubt wanted to know more than Allison wanted to share.

FIFTY

Is it possible to recapture time? To reconstruct experiences and thoughts that shape a life? An unhealthy obsession, revisiting the past. Witnesses retrieve from our archive of denial facts best closeted. Perhaps it's better not to ask questions than evoke unwelcome answers. Sleeping dogs neither bark nor bite left to their untroubled dreams and woe to anyone who disturbs the beast.

Lonely nights on Blanket Hill stirred this cauldron. Out of the enveloping fog of the past voices floated by on winds of memory. Voices that would not be denied.

"You are exacerbating pain," Allison said, her voice soft. Pleading. "It's time to let go. Allow us to return to where we belong."

I turned and gazed at the darkened campus bordering Blanket Hill thinking this is not a night for stars. The sodium vapor glow of street lights blotted out the evening sky.

"And where is that?" I said, addressing shadows. "Where do you belong?"

"In history books," she said. "Forgotten as yesterday's

175

lynchings or like throw-away latch-key children, disregarded. We've become demonized unwashed outlaws rampaging across every TV screen in America, a blood-stained page in our nation's archives that can not be erased, re-cycled, resurrected, or celebrated because the fourth of May would be a day of shame, guilt, or humiliation if the capacity for such feelings survived the obscene degradations we were killed for protesting."

I stared into the surrounding darkness. A gentle breeze caressed my cheek. A familiar scent of cologne stirred memory.

Another voice interrupted my fugue.

"We need forgetfulness," Sandy said. "Not anguish. It's time to end suffering. There's no need to justify how we lived or what we died for. Raising images of the dead bruises wounds that will never heal."

I turned to confront my tormentors thinking these encounters must not continue. Was I on the path to madness? I looked around the hilltop. Black as the night. No one. Nothing. Nada. I prayed I might see something. Someone. A hilltop populated by disembodied voices gave no comfort. I deserved better.

"Goodbye David," Will said. "Your vibes are bad. Real bad. Say goodbye to your fancies; for what really happened on this hill and what is only a memory of what happened? Who knows? Imaginings are not reality. A hundred witnesses can not give back our lives. Really - are we who you say we are?"

"Wait," I shouted into the night. "I don't understand how it happened."

"What's to understand? We are dead. What else

do you need to know?"

"How? Why? A dozen questions."

"Without answers. Believe me, there are no answers. Only more questions. An impossible quest. David, we're worried. What's to become of you?"

"I'll survive."

"Abandon your obsession," Jeff said. "Stop dwelling on what no one but you recalls. Memories are a conspiracy of lies called history and our page was written, approved and closed thirty years ago."

Another voice came out of the night. "Foolish David, fighting ignorance, thinking you can make people see what you see, believe what you believe, feel what you feel. Only denial, massive public-approved denial makes living with horror and guilt possible."

"I can not accept that. I do not agree."

"Get a life, David. Stop scratching dust. Stop blaming yourself because you are alive and we are dead."

Wrong. Without love you can not understand what possessed my imagination. Abandoned on the mountains of the heart I discovered how difficult it is to be loved. More difficult than to give love. And despite pain, to know when it is better to be silent.

How sad there was no time for love to grow into what our love could have become. No time at all.

FIFTY ONE

On Blanket Hill that night Jeff set a melancholy mood. No one spoke a word. Our usual evening chatter vanished as his voice and guitar evoked feelings best expressed in silence. Overhead, Orion the hunter majestically rose from his resting place to climb over the eastern horizon and travel across our sky pursued by contrails tracing shimmering tracks of reflected moonlight.

I, David Constant, committed to Blackstone's Commentaries on the law would prefer to happily spend the rest of my life counting stars. But that, as you know, was not to be.

Was I dreaming? Did these nights, recalled at odd moments, ever exist? My memories and dreams are so entangled each new remembrance raised only unanswered questions. Without doubting sanity I found it hard to believe the dead rise up in my mind to tell me about lives, marriages, families and careers they never had. I found it hard to accept I could recall lives never lived. Difficult, yes. But not impossible. Not when I listened to these young voices enriched with the wonder of just being alive.

"I wanted to live, a life worth living, and I don't mean merely exist," Sandy said quietly addressing only herself.

"I wanted to live - wasn't asking for favors," Jeff sang in reply, strumming a heavy chord on his guitar. "I wanted to live - before I died."

Then, Allison stepped out of the darkness and said, "I wanted to fall deeply, truly in love. I wanted to marry one man, the right man, forever. I wanted to see my child take his first faltering steps. I wanted to pick him up and hold him in my arms when he fell. I wanted to kiss away his tears. Talk away his fears. I wanted to watch his face slowly change with the passing years. Tell me, my friends, was this too much to ask?"

FIFTY TWO

At sunrise a warm breeze gently ruffled window curtains in a dormant Ohio village. Borne on the wind disturbing sounds awakened early risers not with a meadowlark's familiar greeting but by barely audible rumbles some thought a distant thunderstorm or a passing freight train. Citizens peering out bedroom windows saw clouds of black exhaust fumes trailing behind a column of dump trucks eastbound on state highway 10, Kent's main street. A mile-long parade of dirt haulers on oversize tires followed flat-bed trailers transporting bulldozers, back-hoes and power shovels through the town's business district. Their destination; Blanket Hill.

Startled residents returned to bed pulling the covers over their heads asking: My God, what now?

From dawn to dusk morning and afternoon breezes raised dust clouds darkening the sky over Kent State's campus descending on the village like an unwelcome intruder. Walking, playing, working outdoors became difficult. Breathing an agony without surgical masks covering nostrils and mouths. Despite the summer heat windows remained shut, shades down in a futile effort to keep out the pervasive dust.

For a month tailgating trucks grid-locked main street, grinding gears, polluting the air, diesel engines rattling windows as they carried away the bloodstained sod of Blanket Hill. The incessant roar of bulldozers, power shovels and back-hoes leveling the hill became as commonplace as the growl of the firehouse siren at noon. And to the resident's dismay, every morning, despite the previous day's herculean effort to dig, load, and haul away the cursed soil, Blanket Hill remained. Looming high over the hearts and conscience of this troubled Ohio town - forever.

FIFTY THREE

Last night, wandering Blanket Hill in a ROTC uniform Will emerged from the shadows to say in a voice no longer young: "I was the wrong man, in the wrong place at the wrong time."

"You and twelve other students," I said without a smile, turning to answer an apparition more than a memory. Will's face grayed. Old parchment. In the half-light, tears glistened.

"Sandy was killed walking to her next class," I said.

He frowned. "I went to the parking lot to see what was happening."

"And walked right into a Free Fire zone. A real no-brainer. Guardsmen didn't give a damn who they shot."

"Hard to believe." He said, staring. Expressionless eyes. "Hard to believe," he repeated in a hushed voice.

Puzzled. I studied his face. "What's troubling you? Why are you here tonight?"

He shrugged. A long pause. He thought a moment. "I want to see the new health, physical education and recreational facility he said, a surge of anger in

183

his voice. "Can't believe they built a gymnasium on Blanket Hill."

"Seeing's believing." I said, walking away, wanting to end the conversation. Will's appearances were disturbing. I didn't need this. My head was in enough trouble without another miraculous resurrection.

"You can't see the parking lot any more," he said. "Where we were when the guardsmen shot us."

"That's why they built the gym," I replied. "What people can't see anymore couldn't have happened."

Will paused. Shrugged. Then angrily: "It's all been changed. Nothing's here like it was," he said. "Nothing we can remember."

FIFTY FOUR

With Allison and Sandra gone I never married. Never waited outside an obstetric ward to hear "It's a Boy!" or "A Girl!" or possibly "Twins!". Never became a giver and supporter of a new life providing an example of proper conduct to my own child. Never gave identity and coherence to a growing human being. No. Never.

Instead I am now celebrated on "Talk Shows". Barbara Walters, Larry King, and Geraldo beg me to come and boost ratings. Limousines are parked at my door. I dine at the "Four Seasons." Consultants, lawyers and agents offer to show me how to exploit my fifteen minutes of "Fame".

For writing letters Our President never answered?

The media jackals ask: "Why?"

I answer: "Why not?"

Why not remember? Why not recall? Why not learn what happened May 4th 1970?

"The truth shall make thee free" wrote Chaucer in his Ballad of Good Counsel. "Flee from the crowd and dwell with truthfulness," he said. "The crowd has envy - success blinds all."

Right? Right on!

I've recorded every point of view but Our President's.

Abraham Lincoln said: "it is altogether fitting and proper that the living should consecrate and hallow this ground so that our dead will not have died in vain."

Lincoln dedicated a site where a nation's memories resonate. On Blanket Hill a sacred space has been desecrated. On the field of our most recent Civil War a new gymnasium is the ultimate resting place of our nation's denial.

"Lord God of hosts be with us yet.
Lest we forget. Lest we forget."

FIFTY FIVE

There is a pain in the soul pushing us beyond ourselves. Indeed, the wonders of this story rise from hearts sensitized by suffering. Recognize this as well as the facts and you will understand what I am saying is - there is beauty, there is truth, there is God.

Tomorrow's interview will be historic. No voice is more essential than Our President's if there is to be closure.

When the soul of France was stricken a hundred years ago and its citizens divided by hatred, Emile Zola said: "Truth is on the march and nothing will stop her inevitable victory!"

I pray that truth will march for us making reconciliation possible.

Binding a nation's wounds requires an end to contempt. Hatred. Class against class. Race against race. Impossible without the truth that heals. Restorative truth.

Our government violates basic freedoms with impunity unleashing violence against citizens at Kent State, Waco, Ruby Ridge, Detroit, Newark. Handguns, automatic rifles, and AK47s are now inviolable First

Amendment rights. Children traumatized by pervasive killing are today's mass murderers.

Some issues never die until a country makes amends. Injustices fester and become a permanent burden on a nation's soul.

Hopefully, Our President will speak. Answer my questions. For our country is in danger of losing its honor. Tomorrow's interview will clarify a tragic moment in the conscience of a great nation.

FIFTY SIX

The U-shaped metal wand of a security probe slid down my side and between my legs. Our President's imperious secretary examined my brief-case with meticulous care. Convinced I was unarmed he reluctantly returned the appointment card.

"Forget your tape recorder," he said, his voice resonating disapproval. "It will be no use at all."

"I know."

He opened the door to Our President's study and stepped aside. "One hour," he said, pointing to a Nautical clock on the wall. "One hour."

I nodded.

"At four bells, you go!"

The unfriendly gatekeeper followed me into the room. I could feel cold eyes chill the back of my skull.

Sprawled at the foot of our invalid President's chair, Timahoe raised his head. Challenging canine eyes tracked my entry. A wool blanket warmed Our President's legs. He seemed unaware of my approach. Drawn window shades darkened the room. An air conditioner hummed on HIGH. A low flame flickered in the fireplace. Shadows danced on the walls. In one corner the blinking red eye of a security camera monitored my entrance. A writing pad and pencil in Our President's hand seemed poised to again confront the world with incisive prose. I anticipated no exculpatory message from his stroke-afflicted mind.

Timahoe growled. Our President awakened, dark jowls hidden in subdued light. Eyelids fluttered. A familiar demonized image. His furtive look. My list of questions lay untouched on the table. Would nothing but the amnesty of silence prevail today? And tomorrow? Forever? His eyes slowly focused as he emerged from sleep. He nodded at my list and raised one hand in a hospitable "Thumbs-up" salute.

"Thank you for seeing me Mr. President," I said, recalling other images. Campaigner. World Leader. Fallen Idol. A Lion in Winter? Would anyone ever know this man? And, is the knowing all?

A nurse entered carrying a glass. With a conspiratorial wink Our President swallowed his medication grimacing at the taste.

The nurse frowned. "Don't excite the President," she said.

I gave her my most conciliatory nod.

Our President studied comments scribbled in the margins of my letter. He picked up the notepad. Then the pen. Timahoe sprawled on the floor growled a friendly growl. In the fireplace a burning log showered sparks from the hearth. The pungent odor of wood smoke filled the room.

Journey's end.

Our President wrote slowly. His hand steady. "One blink means YES! Two blinks - NO!"

I nodded.

Again he wrote in large block letters:
"A headshake. No Comment!"
I returned a "thumbs up."

His hand trembling, Our President printed his only answers to my questions. Proud. Defiant. Incisive.

His final Statements:

"I AM NOT A CROOK."

"I WAS NOT A MURDERER."

"I REGRET NOTHING."

About The Author

After a 42 year career as a writer-director of many award-winning films and television programs, Norman Weissman has written two novels and a memoir. Determined to oppose the silence in which lies become history, the author makes his reply in art to tell of all he has witnessed during more than half a century of filming at home and overseas.

He lives in rural Connecticut with his wife Eveline, and their little dog Suzie.

Also by Norman Weissman

"Acceptable Losses"
(A Novel)
ISBN-13: 978-0-9801894-0-7

"My Exuberant Voyage"
(A Witness To History)
A Memoir
ISBN-13: 978-0-9801894-3-8

CPSIA information can be obtained at www.ICGtesting.com
Printed in the USA
BVOW04s1948230913

331939BV00001B/17/P